PAPERCUTZ SLICES®

breaking down

"MATURE...
WHEEEE!

PAPERCUTZ™

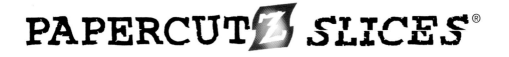

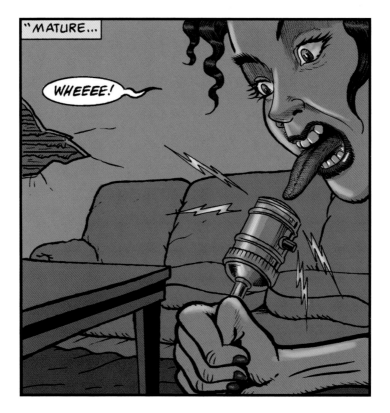

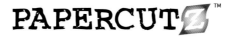

PAPERCUTZ SLICES®

Graphic Novels Available from PAPERCUTZ (Who else..?!)

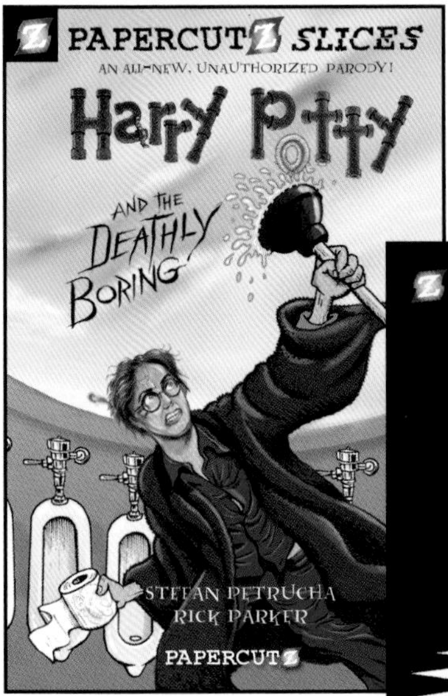
PAPERCUTZ SLICES
AN ALL-NEW, UNAUTHORIZED PARODY!
Harry Potty
AND THE DEATHLY BORING
STEFAN PETRUCHA
RICK PARKER
PAPERCUTZ

Graphic Novel #1
"Harry Potty and
the Deathly Boring"

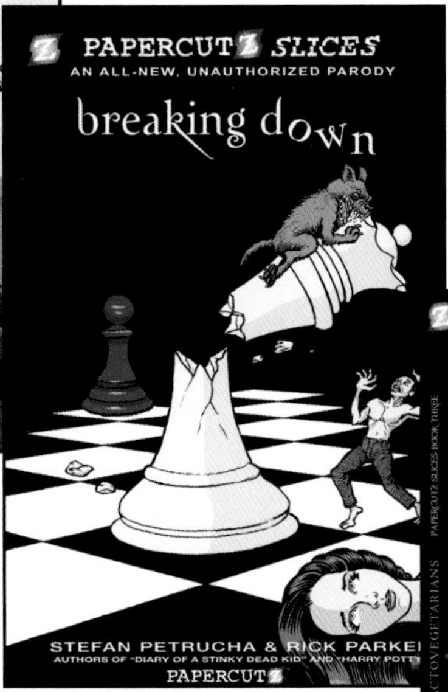
PAPERCUTZ SLICES
AN ALL-NEW, UNAUTHORIZED PARODY
breaking down
STEFAN PETRUCHA & RICK PARKER
PAPERCUTZ

Graphic Novel #2
"Breaking Down"

COMING SOON:
Graphic Novel #3
"Percy Jerkson & The
Ovolactovegetarians"

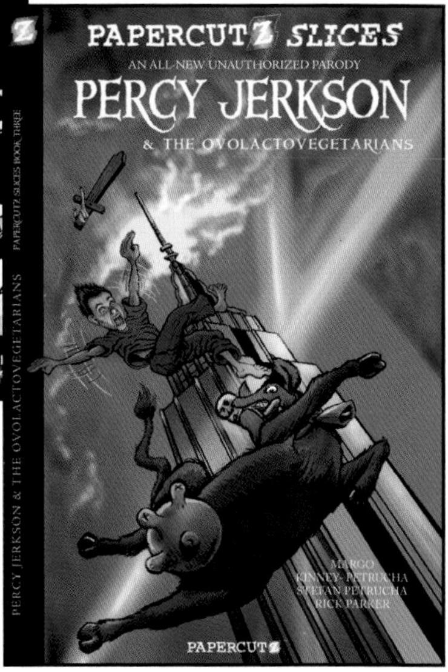
PAPERCUTZ SLICES
AN ALL-NEW UNAUTHORIZED PARODY
PERCY JERKSON
& THE OVOLACTOVEGETARIANS
PERCY JERKSON & THE OVOLACTOVEGETARIANS
PAPERCUTZ

PAPERCUTZ SLICES graphic novels are available at booksellers everywhere. At bookstores, comicbook stores, online, out of the trunk in the back of Rick Parker's car, and who knows where else? If you still are unable to find PAPERCUTZ SLICES (probably because it sold out) you can always order directly from Papercutz—but it'll cost you! PAPERCUTZ SLICES is available in paperback for $6.99 each; in hardcover for $10.99 each. But that's not the worst part-- please add $4.00 for postage and handling for the first book, and add $1.00 for each additional book. Going to your favorite bookseller, buying online, or even getting a copy from your local library doesn't seem so bad now, does it? But if you still insist on ordering from Papercutz, and just to make everything just a little bit more complicated, please make your check payable to NBM Publishing.
Don't ask why—it's just how it works. Send to:

Papercutz, 1200 Country Rd., Rte 523, Flemington, NJ 0822240

Or call 800 886 1223 (9-6 EST M-F)

MC-Visa-Amex accepted

www.papercutz.com

PAPERCUTZ SLICES®

#2 breaking down

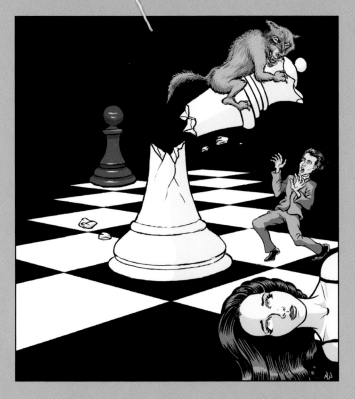

MAIA KINNEY-PETRUCHA & STEFAN PETRUCHA
Writers
RICK PARKER
Artist

New York

"breaking down"

MAIA KINNEY-PETRUCHA & STEFAN PETRUCHA – Writers
RICK PARKER – Artist

SHELLY STERNER & CHRIS NELSON
Production

MICHAEL PETRANEK
Associate Editor

JIM SALICRUP
Editor-in-Chief

ISBN: 978-1-59707-244-1 paperback edition
ISBN: 978-1-59707-245-8 hardcover edition

Printed in Hong Kong
January 2011 by New Era Printing LTD
Trend Centre, 29-31 Cheung Lee St.
Rm. 1101-1103, 11/F
Chaiwan, Hong Kong

First Printing

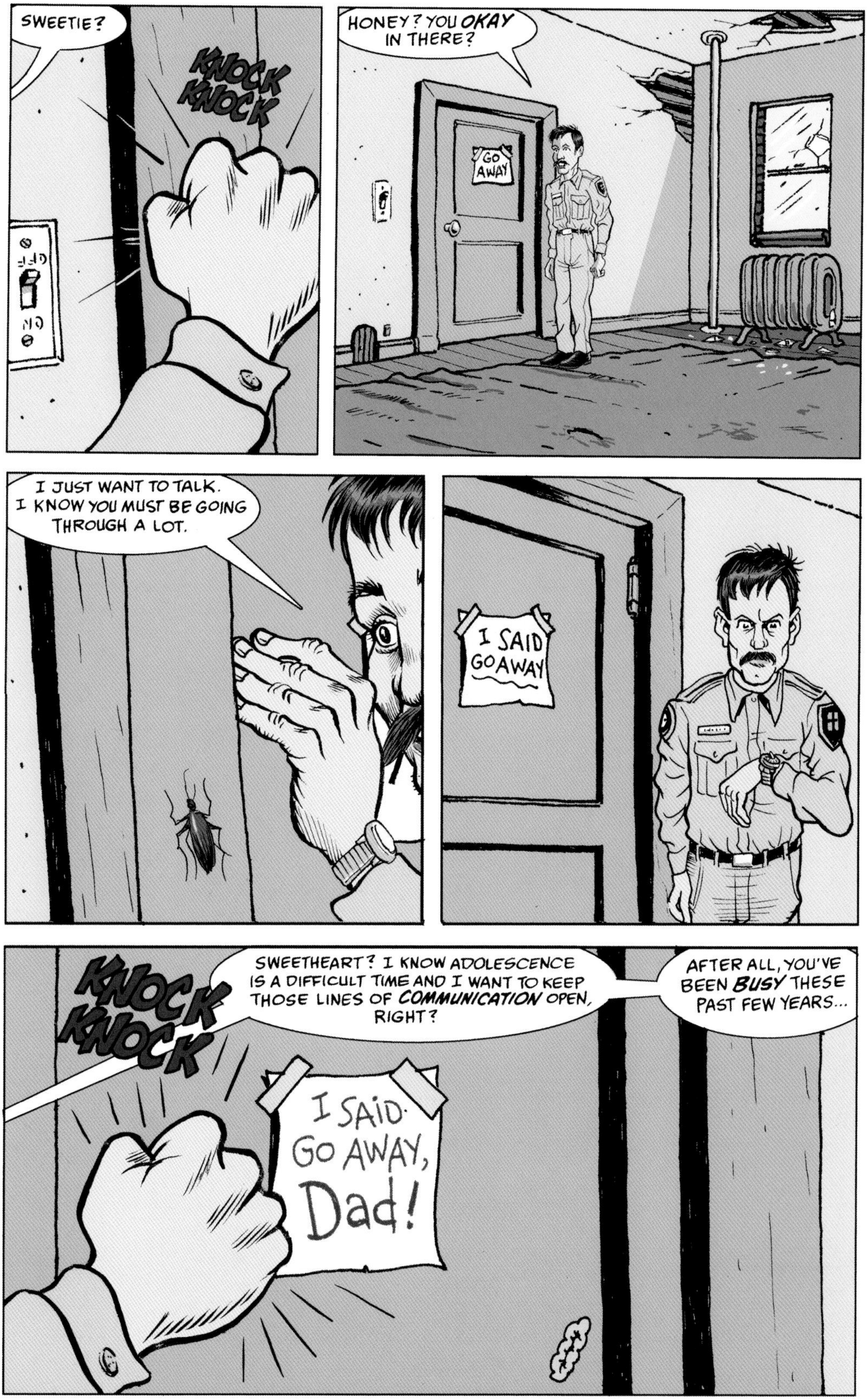
SWEETIE?
KNOCK KNOCK
OFF
ON
HONEY? YOU OKAY IN THERE?
GO AWAY
I JUST WANT TO TALK. I KNOW YOU MUST BE GOING THROUGH A LOT.
I SAID GO AWAY
KNOCK KNOCK
SWEETHEART? I KNOW ADOLESCENCE IS A DIFFICULT TIME AND I WANT TO KEEP THOSE LINES OF COMMUNICATION OPEN, RIGHT?
AFTER ALL, YOU'VE BEEN BUSY THESE PAST FEW YEARS...
I SAID GO AWAY, Dad!

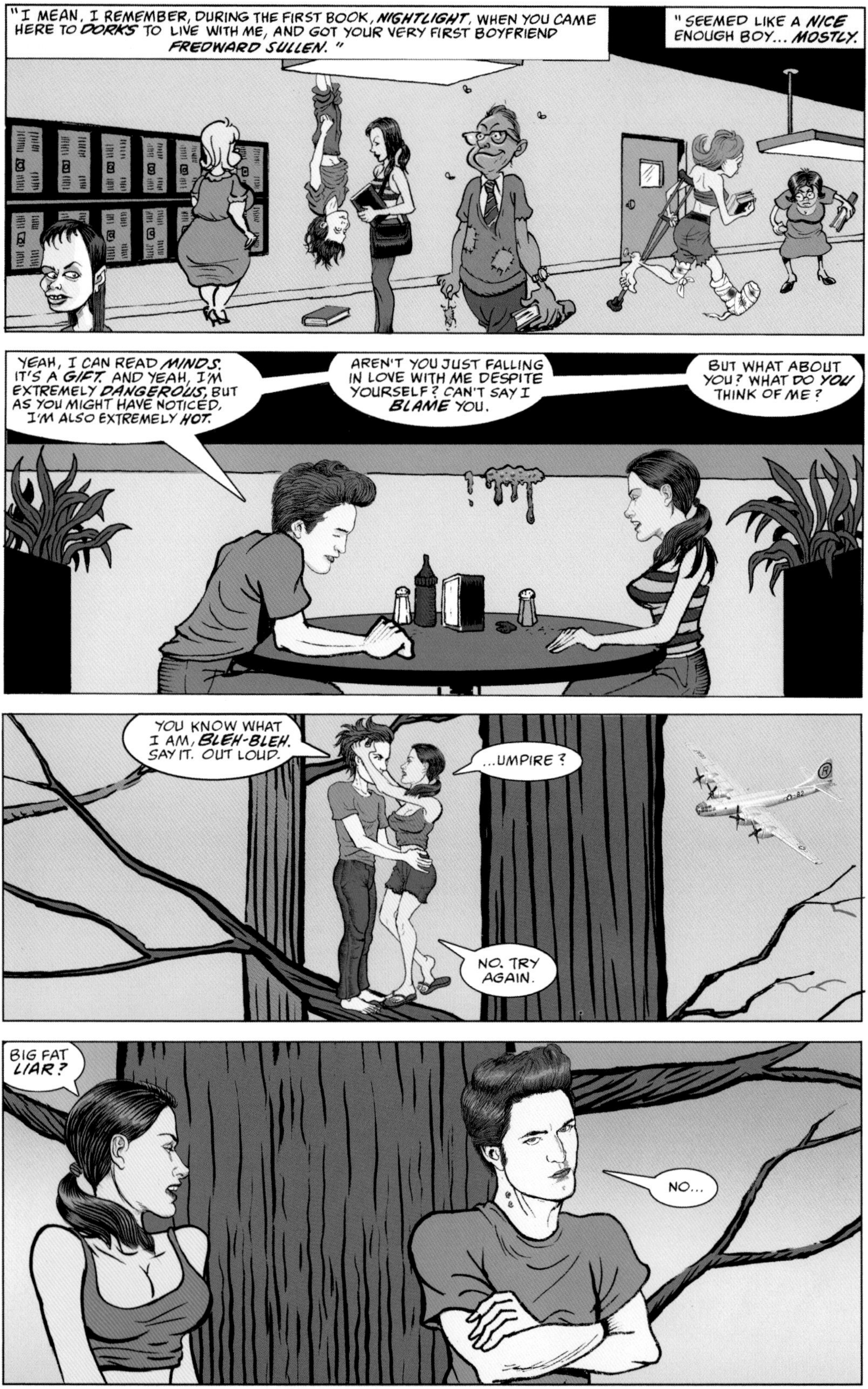
"I MEAN, I REMEMBER, DURING THE FIRST BOOK, NIGHTLIGHT, WHEN YOU CAME HERE TO DORKS TO LIVE WITH ME, AND GOT YOUR VERY FIRST BOYFRIEND FREDWARD SULLEN."
"SEEMED LIKE A NICE ENOUGH BOY... MOSTLY.
YEAH, I CAN READ MINDS. IT'S A GIFT. AND YEAH, I'M EXTREMELY DANGEROUS, BUT AS YOU MIGHT HAVE NOTICED, I'M ALSO EXTREMELY HOT.
AREN'T YOU JUST FALLING IN LOVE WITH ME DESPITE YOURSELF? CAN'T SAY I BLAME YOU.
BUT WHAT ABOUT YOU? WHAT DO YOU THINK OF ME?
YOU KNOW WHAT I AM, BLEH-BLEH. SAY IT. OUT LOUD.
...UMPIRE?
NO. TRY AGAIN.
BIG FAT LIAR?
NO...

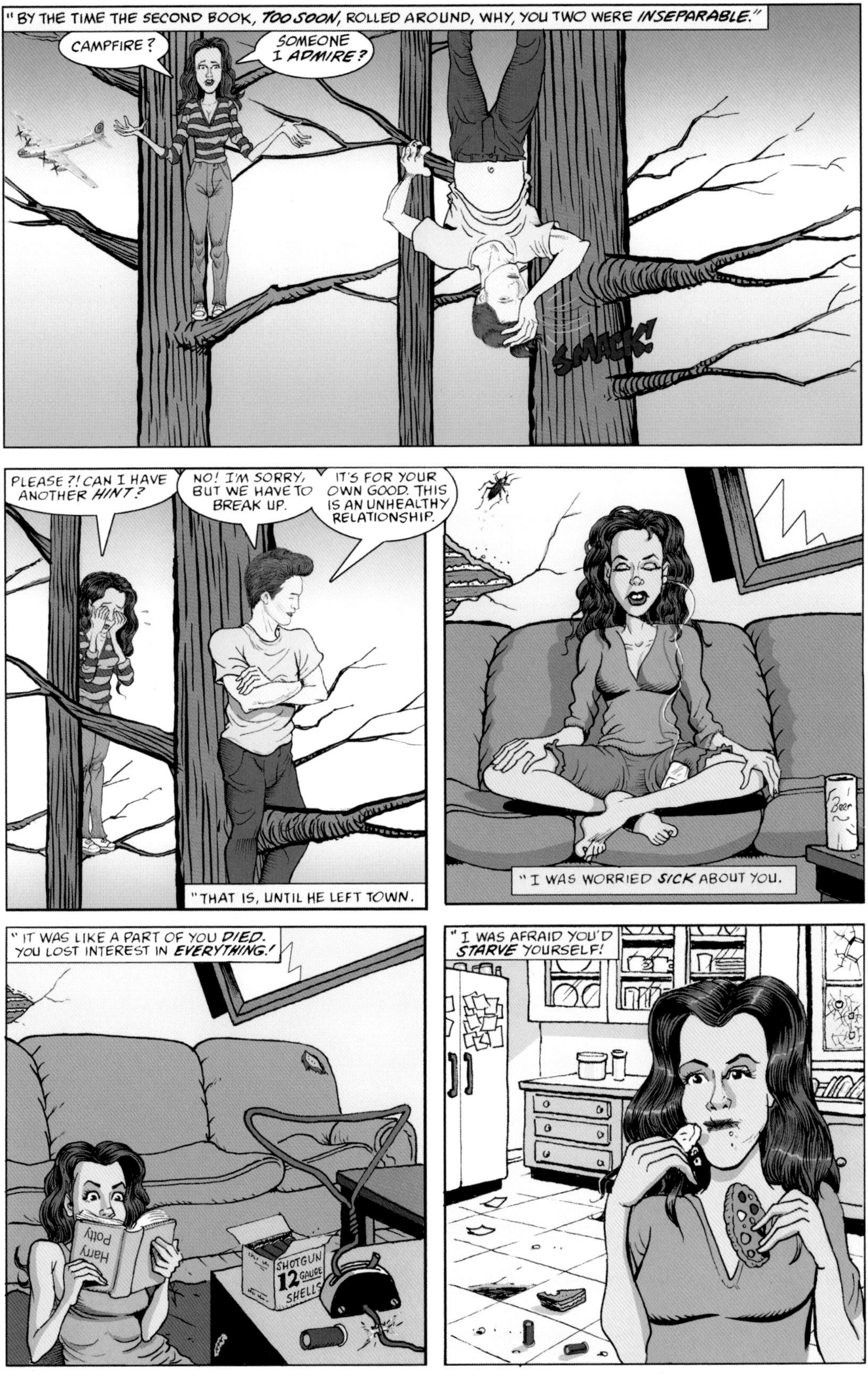
"BY THE TIME THE SECOND BOOK, TOO SOON, ROLLED AROUND, WHY, YOU TWO WERE INSEPARABLE."
CAMPFIRE?
SOMEONE I ADMIRE?
SMACK!
PLEASE?! CAN I HAVE ANOTHER HINT?
NO! I'M SORRY, BUT WE HAVE TO BREAK UP.
IT'S FOR YOUR OWN GOOD. THIS IS AN UNHEALTHY RELATIONSHIP.
"THAT IS, UNTIL HE LEFT TOWN.
Beer
"I WAS WORRIED SICK ABOUT YOU.
"IT WAS LIKE A PART OF YOU DIED. YOU LOST INTEREST IN EVERYTHING!
Harry Potty
SHOTGUN 12 GAUGE SHELLS
"I WAS AFRAID YOU'D STARVE YOURSELF!

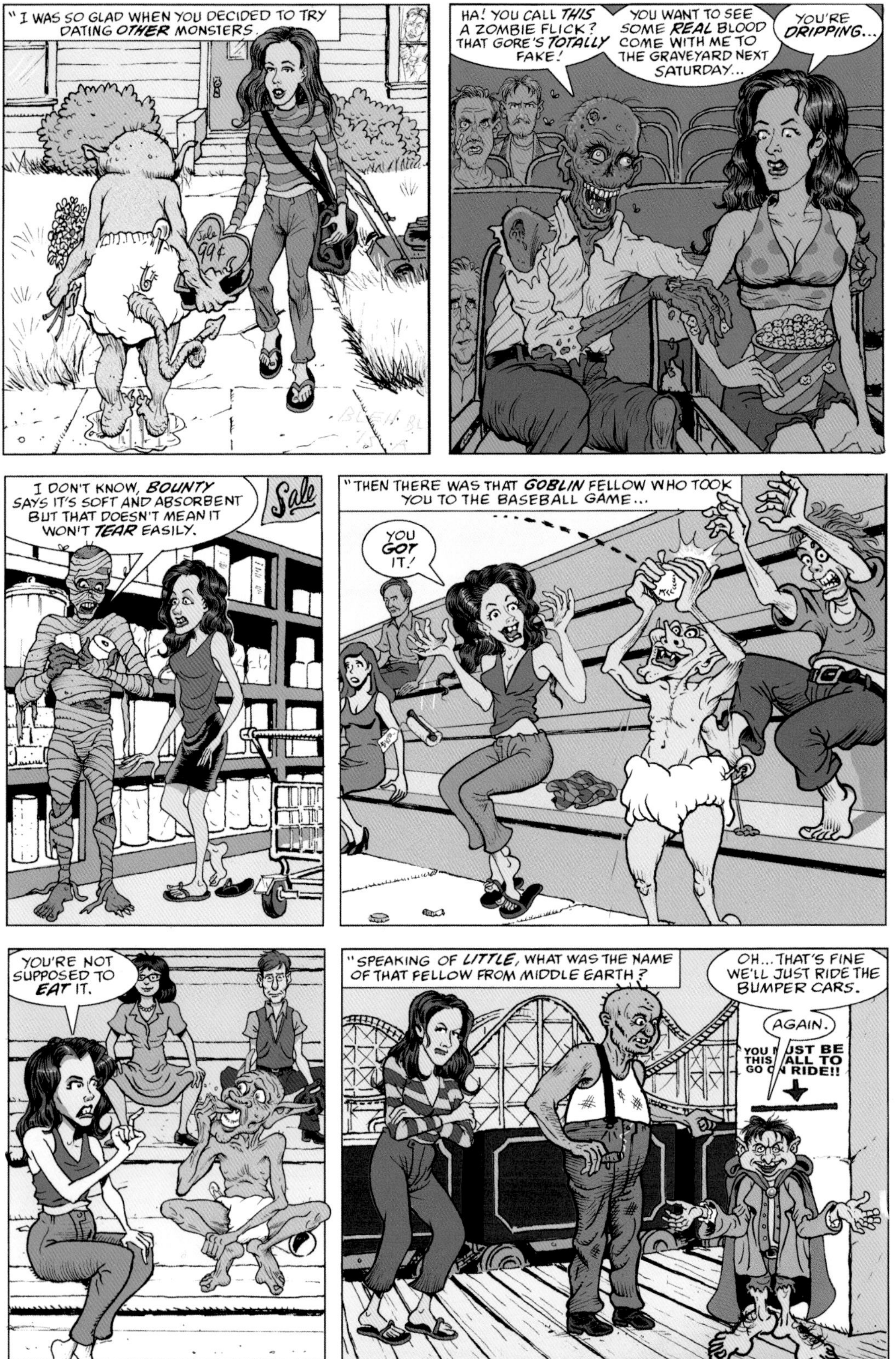
"I WAS SO GLAD WHEN YOU DECIDED TO TRY DATING OTHER MONSTERS.
Sale 99¢
HA! YOU CALL THIS A ZOMBIE FLICK? THAT GORE'S TOTALLY FAKE!
YOU WANT TO SEE SOME REAL BLOOD COME WITH ME TO THE GRAVEYARD NEXT SATURDAY...
YOU'RE DRIPPING...
I DON'T KNOW, BOUNTY SAYS IT'S SOFT AND ABSORBENT BUT THAT DOESN'T MEAN IT WON'T TEAR EASILY.
Sale
"THEN THERE WAS THAT GOBLIN FELLOW WHO TOOK YOU TO THE BASEBALL GAME...
YOU GOT IT!
YOU'RE NOT SUPPOSED TO EAT IT.
" BUT I GUESS THE LITTLE FELLOW HAD TROUBLE ASSIMILATING OUR CULTURE.
"SPEAKING OF LITTLE, WHAT WAS THE NAME OF THAT FELLOW FROM MIDDLE EARTH?
OH... THAT'S FINE WE'LL JUST RIDE THE BUMPER CARS.
AGAIN.
YOU UST BE THIS ALL TO GO O RIDE!!

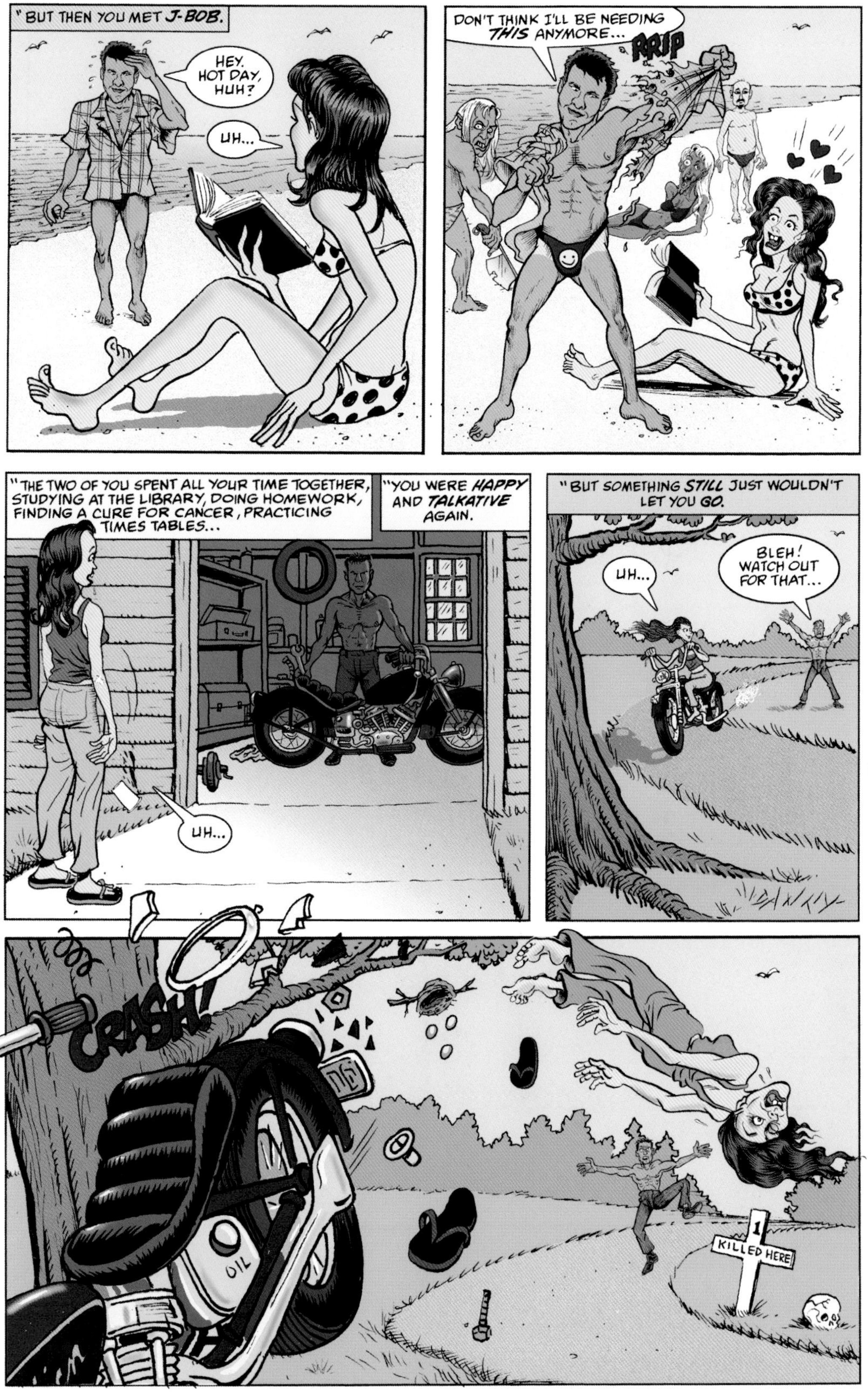
"BUT THEN YOU MET J-BOB.
HEY. HOT DAY, HUH?
UH...
DON'T THINK I'LL BE NEEDING THIS ANYMORE...
RRIP
"THE TWO OF YOU SPENT ALL YOUR TIME TOGETHER, STUDYING AT THE LIBRARY, DOING HOMEWORK, FINDING A CURE FOR CANCER, PRACTICING TIMES TABLES...
"YOU WERE HAPPY AND TALKATIVE AGAIN.
UH...
"BUT SOMETHING STILL JUST WOULDN'T LET YOU GO.
UH...
BLEH! WATCH OUT FOR THAT...
CRASH!
OIL
1
KILLED HERE

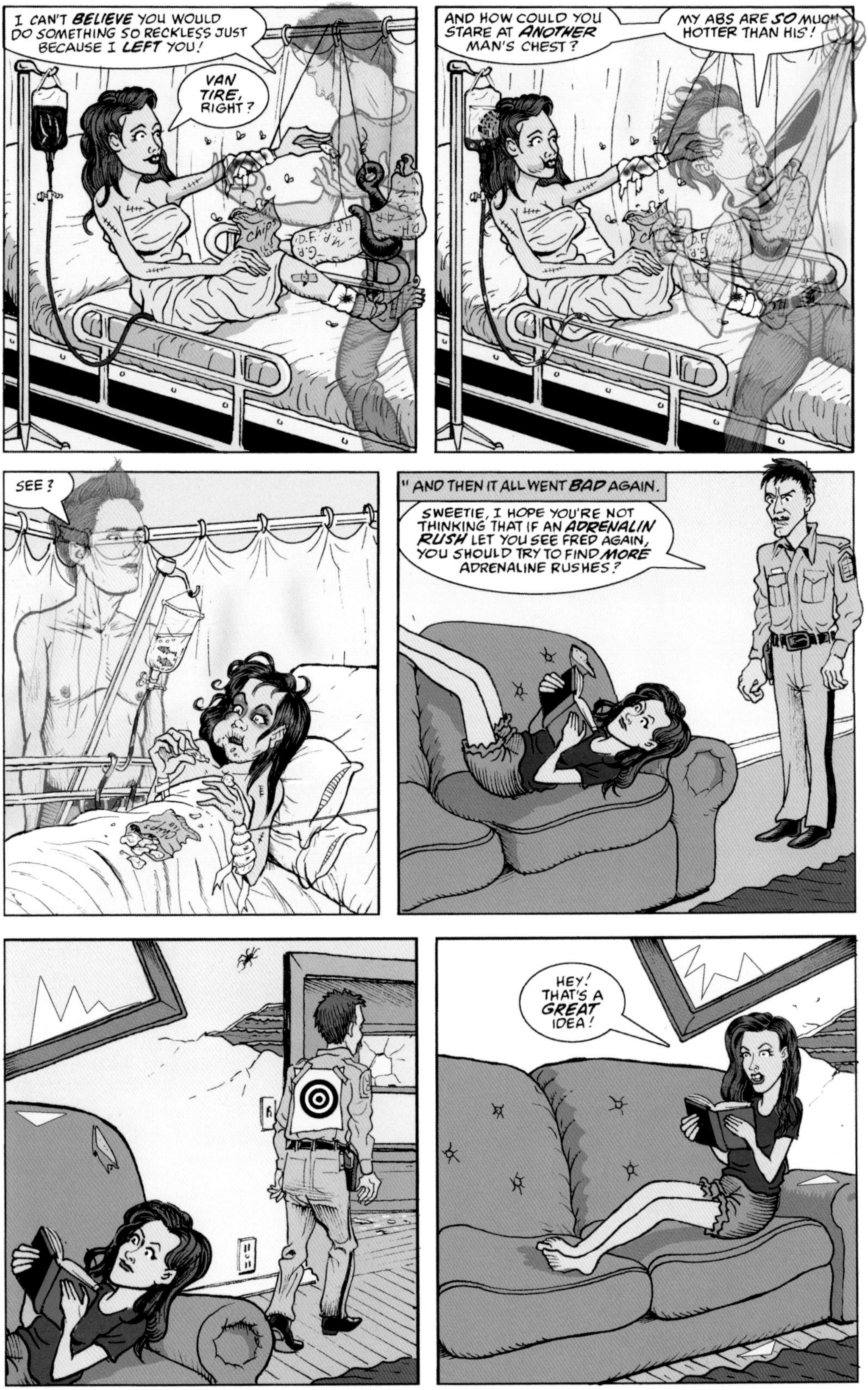
I CAN'T BELIEVE YOU WOULD DO SOMETHING SO RECKLESS JUST BECAUSE I LEFT YOU!
VAN TIRE, RIGHT?
AND HOW COULD YOU STARE AT ANOTHER MAN'S CHEST?
MY ABS ARE SO MUCH HOTTER THAN HIS!
SEE?
"AND THEN IT ALL WENT BAD AGAIN.
SWEETIE, I HOPE YOU'RE NOT THINKING THAT IF AN ADRENALIN RUSH LET YOU SEE FRED AGAIN, YOU SHOULD TRY TO FIND MORE ADRENALINE RUSHES?
HEY! THAT'S A GREAT IDEA!

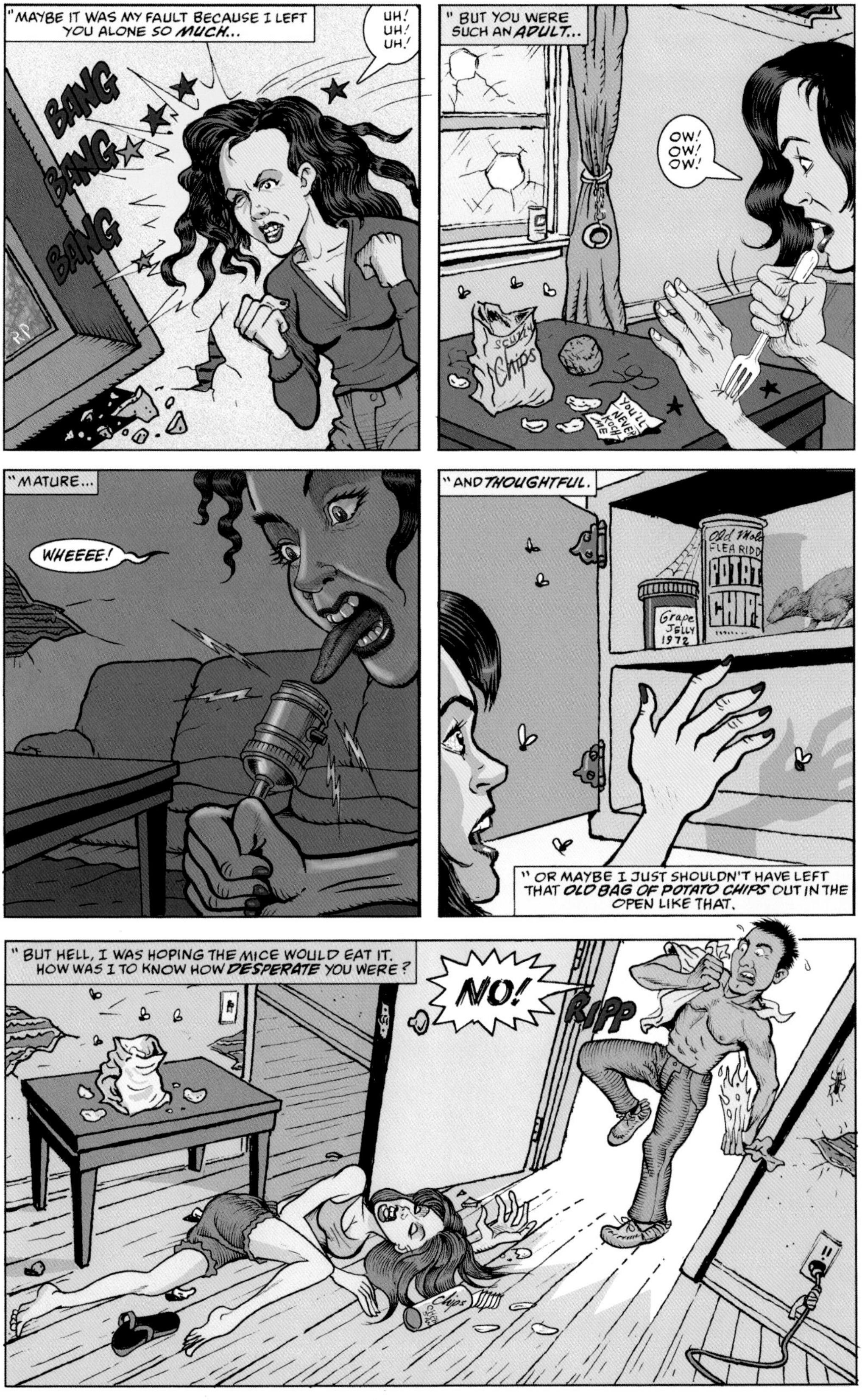
"MAYBE IT WAS MY FAULT BECAUSE I LEFT YOU ALONE SO MUCH...
UH! UH! UH!
BANG
BANG
BANG
"BUT YOU WERE SUCH AN ADULT...
OW! OW! OW!
Chips
"MATURE...
WHEEEE!
"AND THOUGHTFUL.
Grape JELLY 1972
"OR MAYBE I JUST SHOULDN'T HAVE LEFT THAT OLD BAG OF POTATO CHIPS OUT IN THE OPEN LIKE THAT.
"BUT HELL, I WAS HOPING THE MICE WOULD EAT IT. HOW WAS I TO KNOW HOW DESPERATE YOU WERE?
NO!
RIPP
Chips

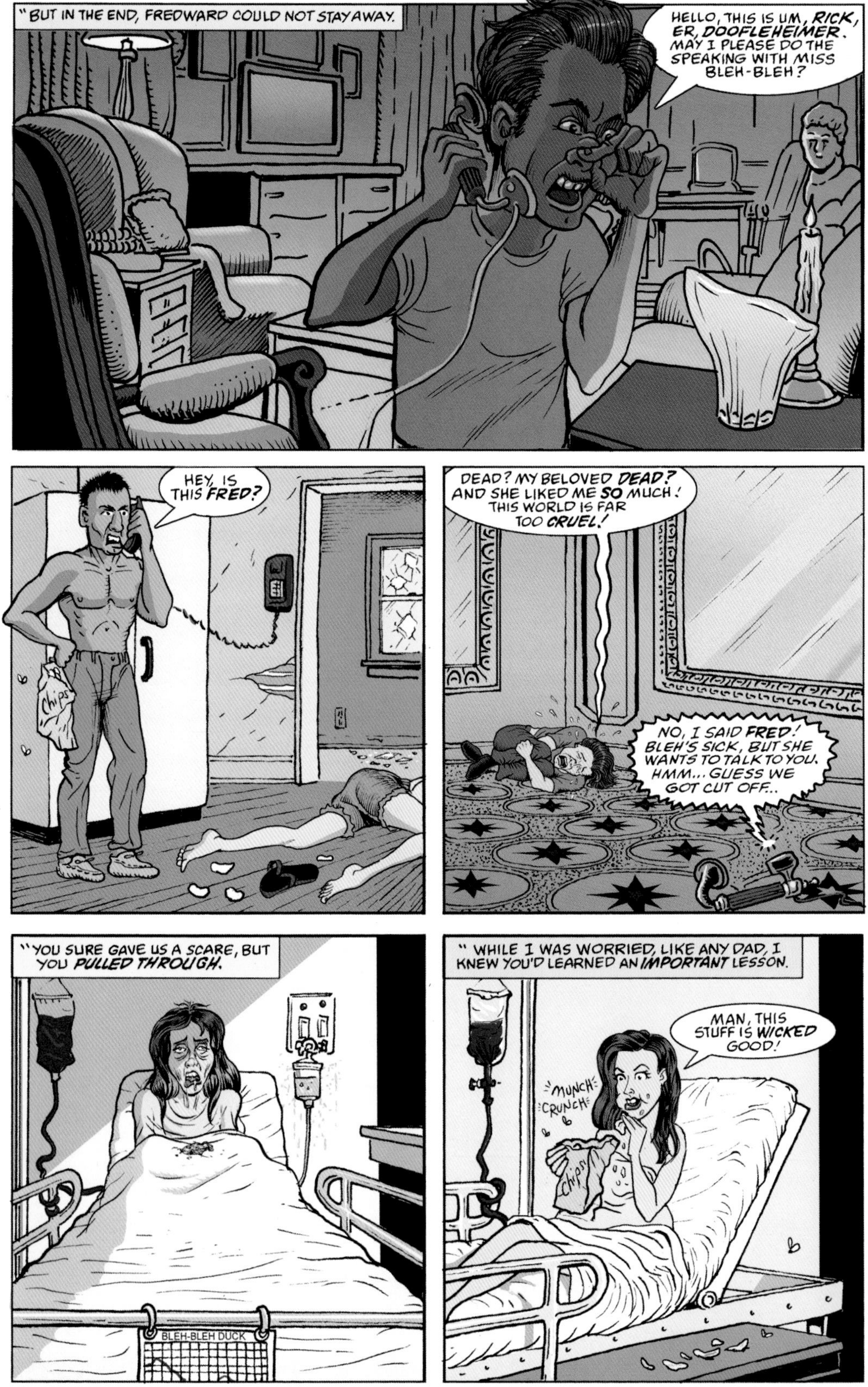
"BUT IN THE END, FREDWARD COULD NOT STAY AWAY.
HELLO, THIS IS UM, RICK, ER, DOOFLEHEIMER. MAY I PLEASE DO THE SPEAKING WITH MISS BLEH-BLEH?
HEY, IS THIS FRED?
CHIPS
DEAD? MY BELOVED DEAD? AND SHE LIKED ME SO MUCH! THIS WORLD IS FAR TOO CRUEL!
NO, I SAID FRED! BLEH'S SICK, BUT SHE WANTS TO TALK TO YOU. HMM... GUESS WE GOT CUT OFF..
"YOU SURE GAVE US A SCARE, BUT YOU PULLED THROUGH.
BLEH-BLEH DUCK
"WHILE I WAS WORRIED, LIKE ANY DAD, I KNEW YOU'D LEARNED AN IMPORTANT LESSON.
MAN, THIS STUFF IS WICKED GOOD!
MUNCH
CRUNCH
CHIPS

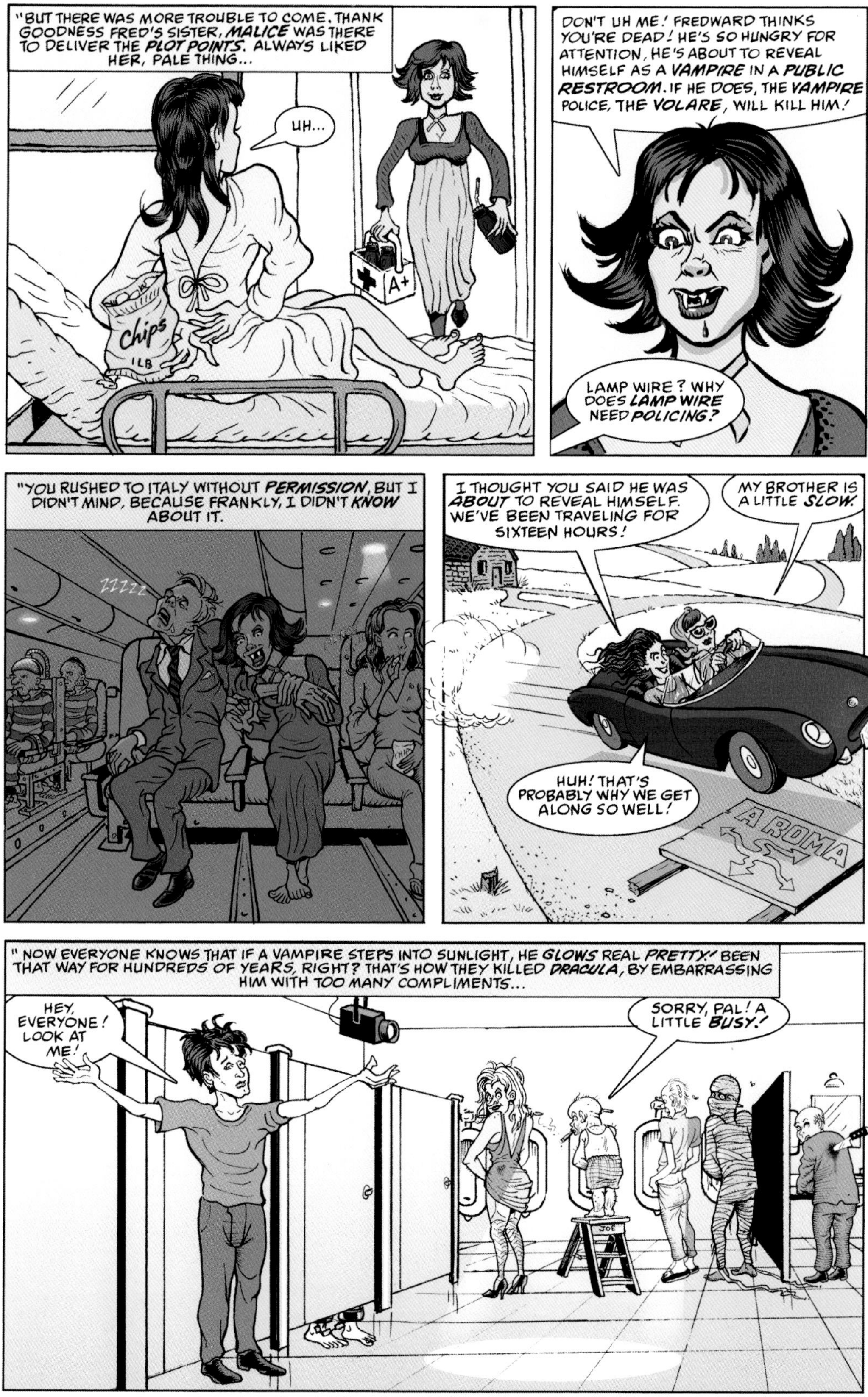
"BUT THERE WAS MORE TROUBLE TO COME. THANK GOODNESS FRED'S SISTER, MALICE WAS THERE TO DELIVER THE PLOT POINTS. ALWAYS LIKED HER, PALE THING...
UH...
Chips
1LB
A+
DON'T UH ME! FREDWARD THINKS YOU'RE DEAD! HE'S SO HUNGRY FOR ATTENTION, HE'S ABOUT TO REVEAL HIMSELF AS A VAMPIRE IN A PUBLIC RESTROOM. IF HE DOES, THE VAMPIRE POLICE, THE VOLARE, WILL KILL HIM!
LAMP WIRE? WHY DOES LAMP WIRE NEED POLICING?
"YOU RUSHED TO ITALY WITHOUT PERMISSION, BUT I DIDN'T MIND, BECAUSE FRANKLY, I DIDN'T KNOW ABOUT IT.
ZZZZZ
I THOUGHT YOU SAID HE WAS ABOUT TO REVEAL HIMSELF. WE'VE BEEN TRAVELING FOR SIXTEEN HOURS!
MY BROTHER IS A LITTLE SLOW.
HUH! THAT'S PROBABLY WHY WE GET ALONG SO WELL!
A ROMA
" NOW EVERYONE KNOWS THAT IF A VAMPIRE STEPS INTO SUNLIGHT, HE GLOWS REAL PRETTY! BEEN THAT WAY FOR HUNDREDS OF YEARS, RIGHT? THAT'S HOW THEY KILLED DRACULA, BY EMBARRASSING HIM WITH TOO MANY COMPLIMENTS...
HEY, EVERYONE! LOOK AT ME!
SORRY, PAL! A LITTLE BUSY!
JOE

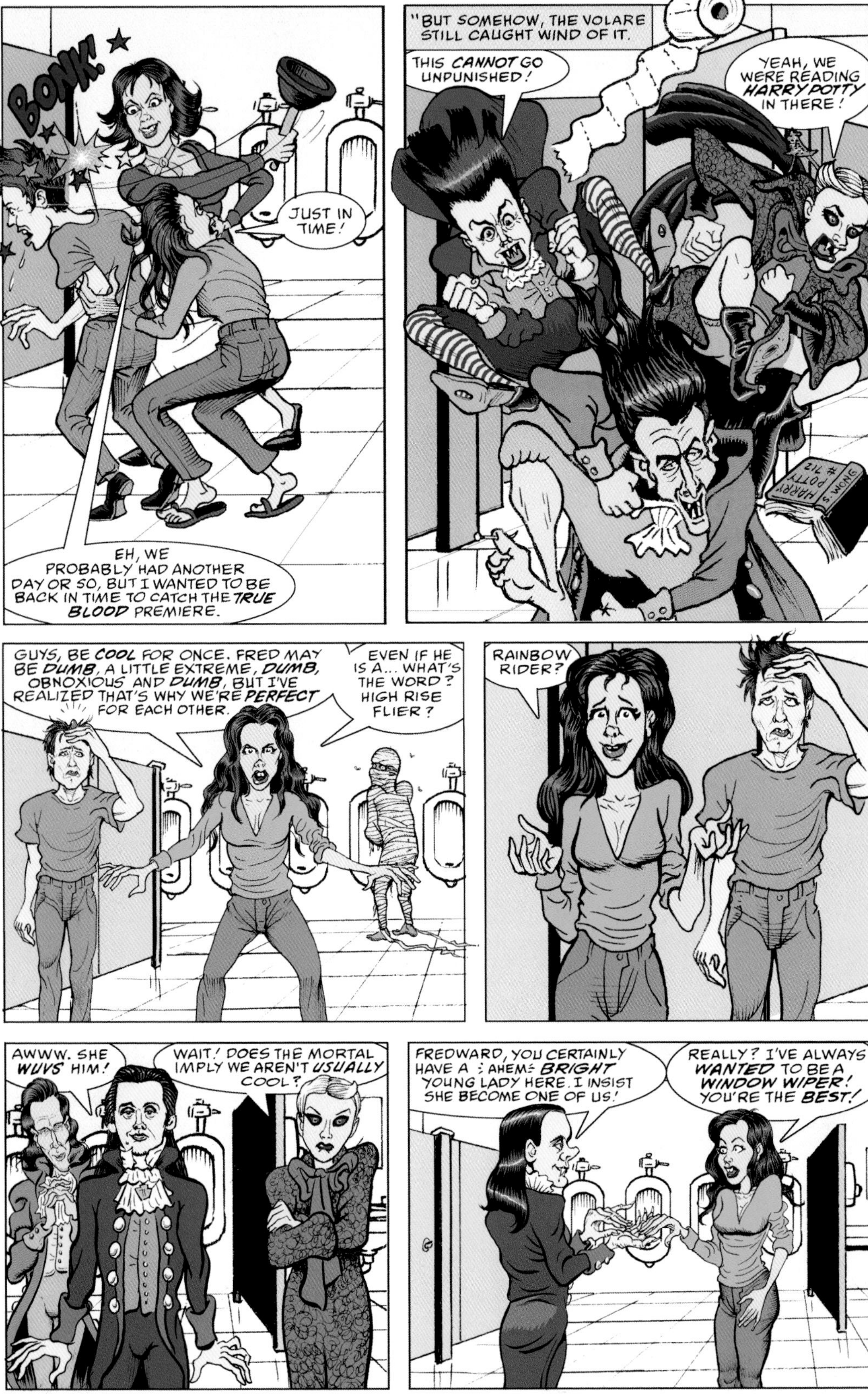
BONK!
JUST IN TIME!
EH, WE PROBABLY HAD ANOTHER DAY OR SO, BUT I WANTED TO BE BACK IN TIME TO CATCH THE TRUE BLOOD PREMIERE.
"BUT SOMEHOW, THE VOLARE STILL CAUGHT WIND OF IT.
THIS CANNOT GO UNPUNISHED!
YEAH, WE WERE READING HARRY POTTY IN THERE!
HARRY POTTY #712
GUYS, BE COOL FOR ONCE. FRED MAY BE DUMB, A LITTLE EXTREME, DUMB, OBNOXIOUS AND DUMB, BUT I'VE REALIZED THAT'S WHY WE'RE PERFECT FOR EACH OTHER.
EVEN IF HE IS A... WHAT'S THE WORD? HIGH RISE FLIER?
RAINBOW RIDER?
AWWW. SHE WUVS HIM!
WAIT! DOES THE MORTAL IMPLY WE AREN'T USUALLY COOL?
FREDWARD, YOU CERTAINLY HAVE A :AHEM: BRIGHT YOUNG LADY HERE. I INSIST SHE BECOME ONE OF US!
REALLY? I'VE ALWAYS WANTED TO BE A WINDOW WIPER! YOU'RE THE BEST!

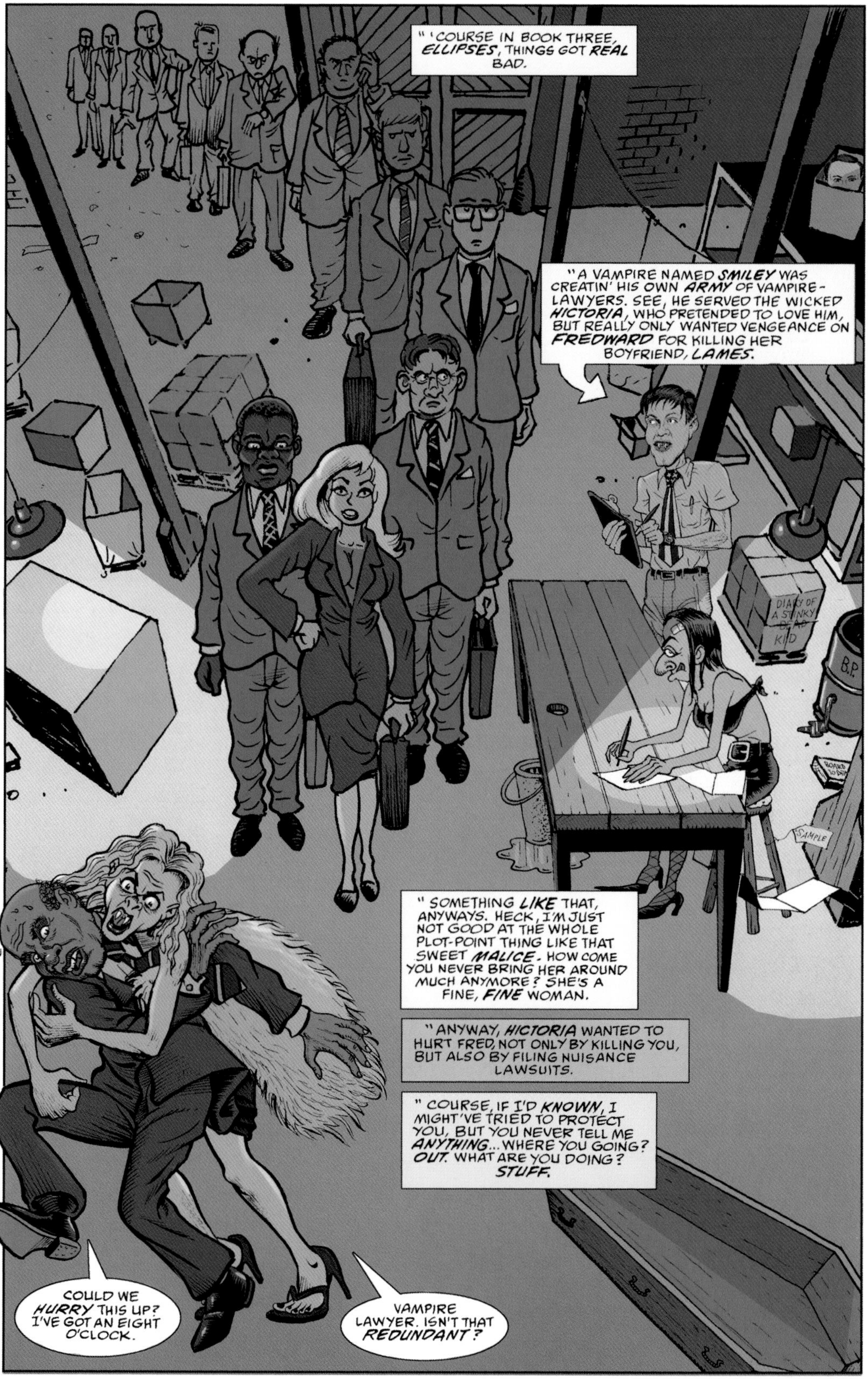
"'COURSE IN BOOK THREE, ELLIPSES, THINGS GOT REAL BAD.
"A VAMPIRE NAMED SMILEY WAS CREATIN' HIS OWN ARMY OF VAMPIRE-LAWYERS. SEE, HE SERVED THE WICKED HICTORIA, WHO PRETENDED TO LOVE HIM, BUT REALLY ONLY WANTED VENGEANCE ON FREDWARD FOR KILLING HER BOYFRIEND, LAMES.
DIARY OF A STINKY DEAD KID
B.P.
SAMPLE
"SOMETHING LIKE THAT, ANYWAYS. HECK, I'M JUST NOT GOOD AT THE WHOLE PLOT-POINT THING LIKE THAT SWEET MALICE. HOW COME YOU NEVER BRING HER AROUND MUCH ANYMORE? SHE'S A FINE, FINE WOMAN.
"ANYWAY, HICTORIA WANTED TO HURT FRED, NOT ONLY BY KILLING YOU, BUT ALSO BY FILING NUISANCE LAWSUITS.
"COURSE, IF I'D KNOWN, I MIGHT'VE TRIED TO PROTECT YOU, BUT YOU NEVER TELL ME ANYTHING... WHERE YOU GOING? OUT. WHAT ARE YOU DOING? STUFF.
COULD WE HURRY THIS UP? I'VE GOT AN EIGHT O'CLOCK.
VAMPIRE LAWYER. ISN'T THAT REDUNDANT?

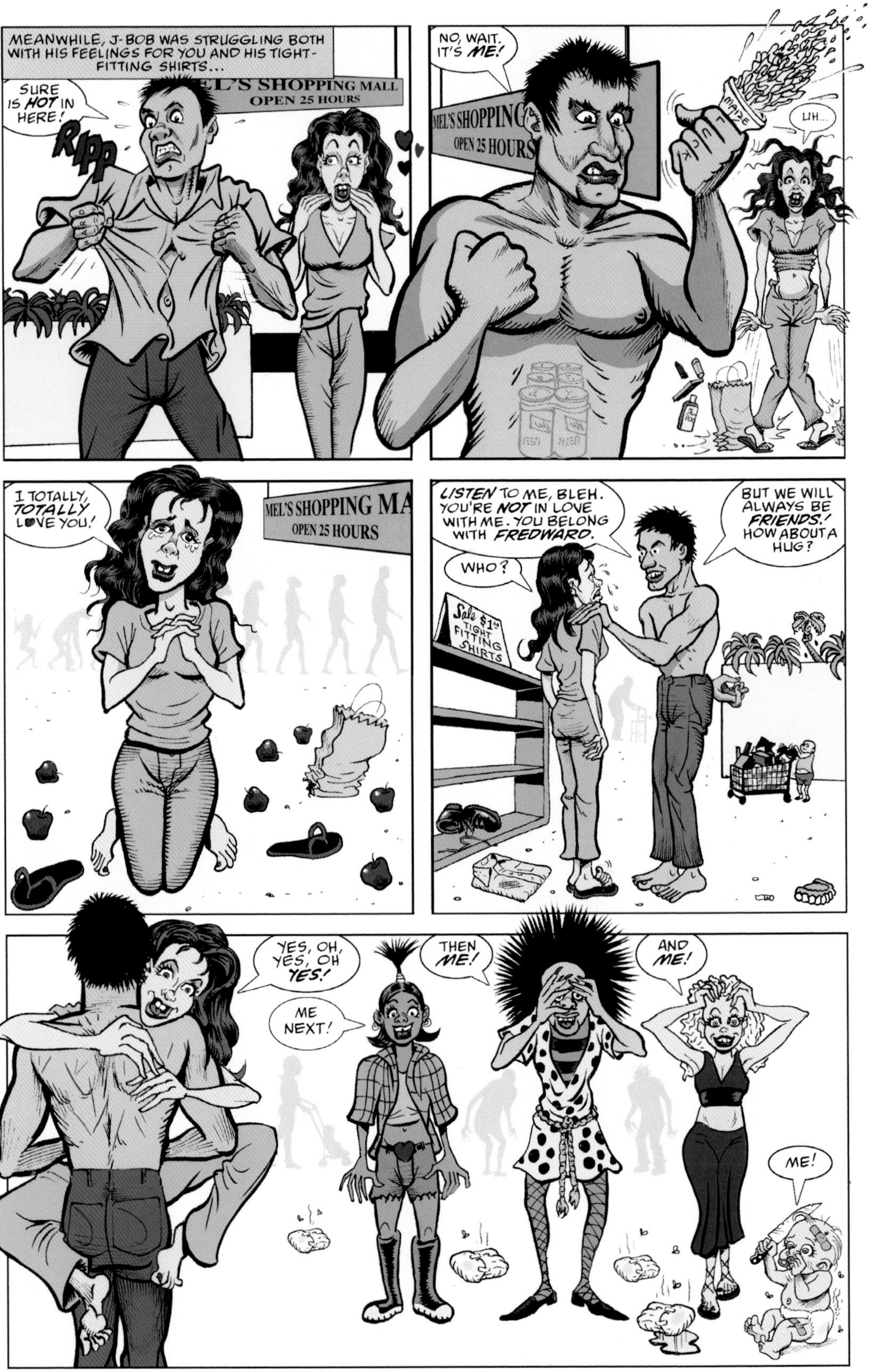
MEANWHILE, J-BOB WAS STRUGGLING BOTH WITH HIS FEELINGS FOR YOU AND HIS TIGHT-FITTING SHIRTS...
EL'S SHOPPING MALL
OPEN 25 HOURS
SURE IS HOT IN HERE!
RIPP
NO, WAIT. IT'S ME!
MEL'S SHOPPING
OPEN 25 HOURS
UH...
I TOTALLY, TOTALLY LOVE YOU!
MEL'S SHOPPING MA
OPEN 25 HOURS
LISTEN TO ME, BLEH. YOU'RE NOT IN LOVE WITH ME. YOU BELONG WITH FREDWARD.
WHO?
BUT WE WILL ALWAYS BE FRIENDS! HOW ABOUT A HUG?
Sale $1
TIGHT FITTING SHIRTS
YES, OH, YES, OH YES!
ME NEXT!
THEN ME!
AND ME!
ME!

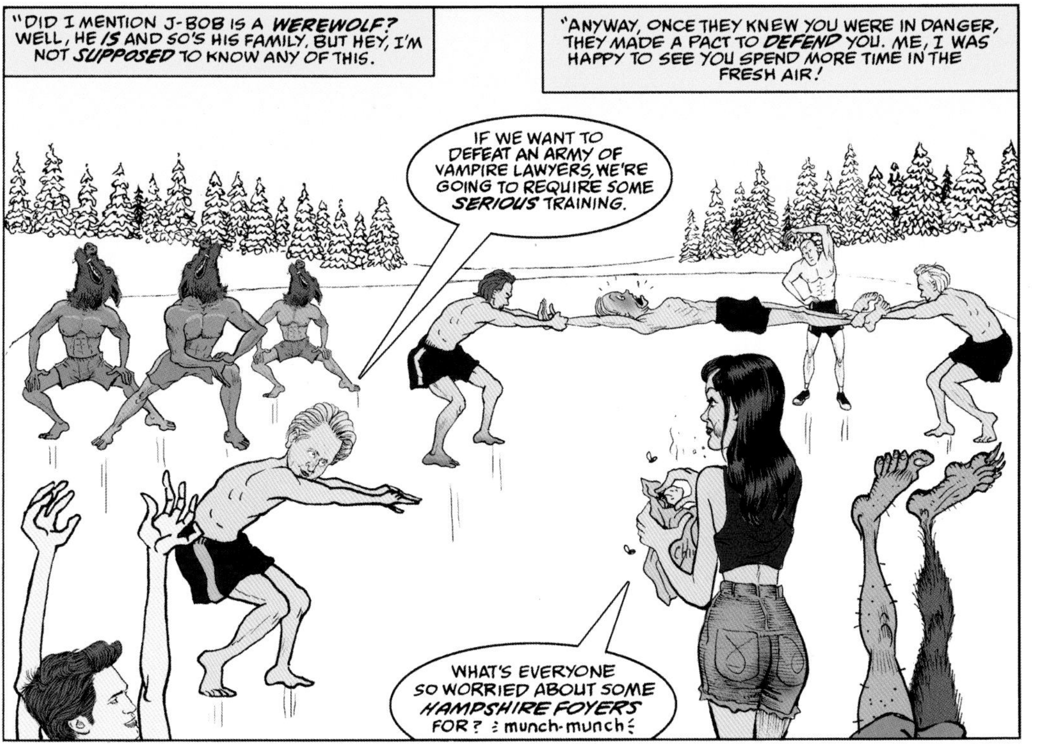
"DID I MENTION J-BOB IS A WEREWOLF? WELL, HE IS AND SO'S HIS FAMILY. BUT HEY, I'M NOT SUPPOSED TO KNOW ANY OF THIS.
"ANYWAY, ONCE THEY KNEW YOU WERE IN DANGER, THEY MADE A PACT TO DEFEND YOU. ME, I WAS HAPPY TO SEE YOU SPEND MORE TIME IN THE FRESH AIR!
IF WE WANT TO DEFEAT AN ARMY OF VAMPIRE LAWYERS, WE'RE GOING TO REQUIRE SOME SERIOUS TRAINING.
WHAT'S EVERYONE SO WORRIED ABOUT SOME HAMPSHIRE FOYERS FOR? munch-munch

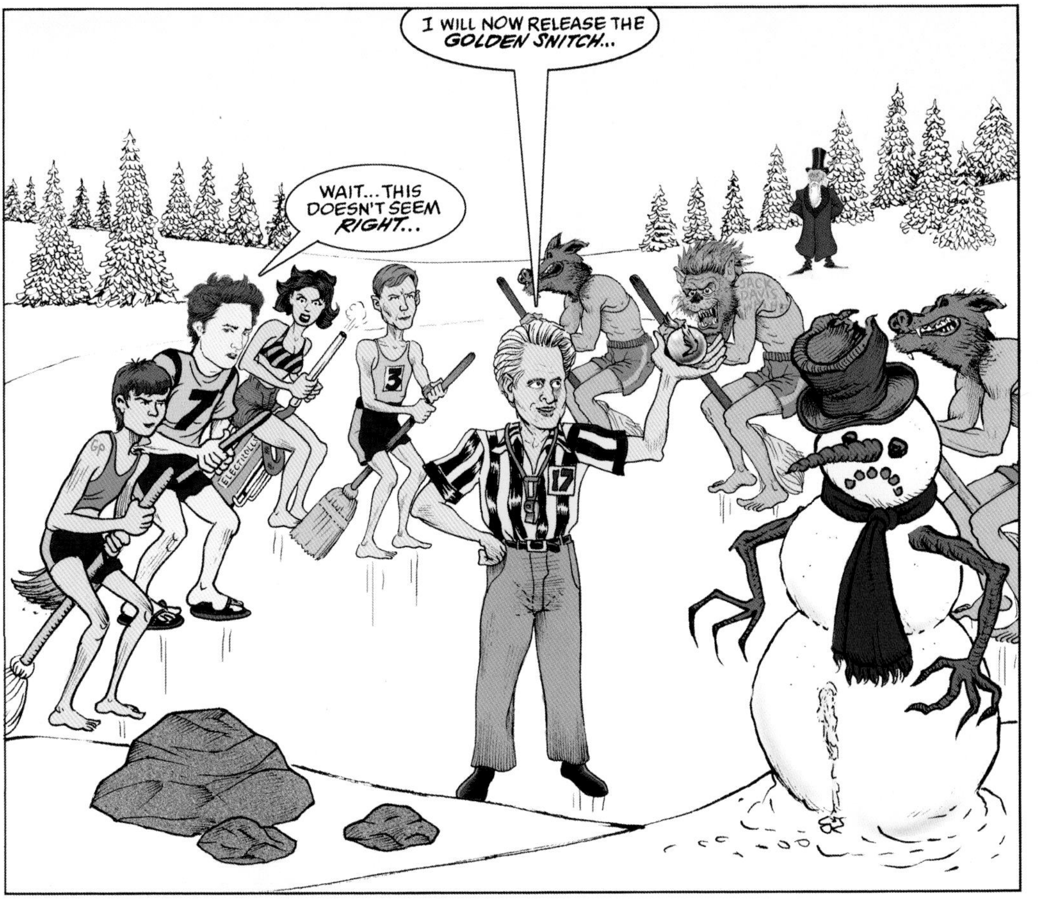
I WILL NOW RELEASE THE GOLDEN SNITCH...
WAIT... THIS DOESN'T SEEM RIGHT...

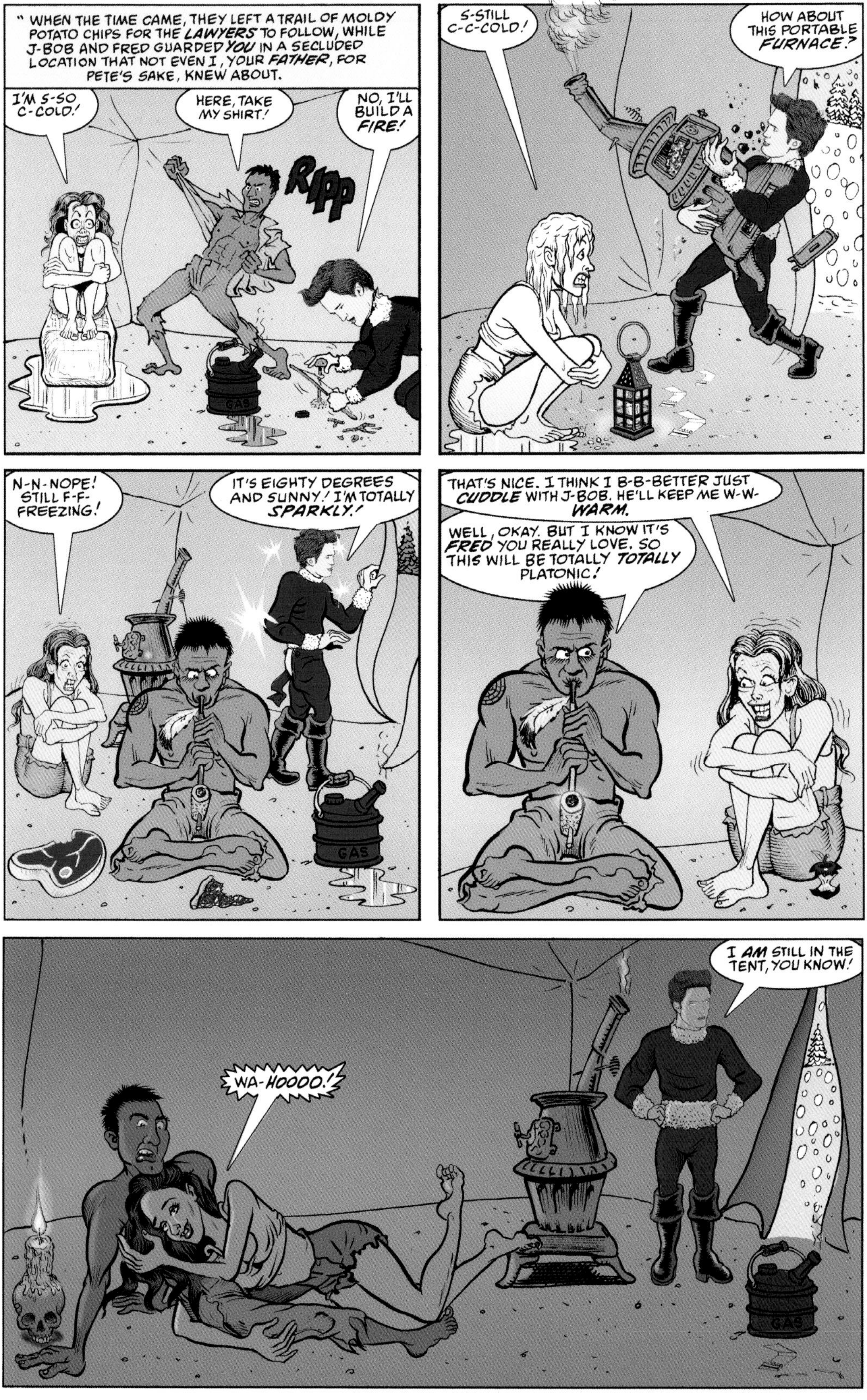

"WHEN THE TIME CAME, THEY LEFT A TRAIL OF MOLDY POTATO CHIPS FOR THE *LAWYERS* TO FOLLOW, WHILE J-BOB AND FRED GUARDED *YOU* IN A SECLUDED LOCATION THAT NOT EVEN I, YOUR *FATHER*, FOR PETE'S SAKE, KNEW ABOUT.
I'M S-SO C-COLD!
HERE, TAKE MY SHIRT!
RIPP
NO, I'LL BUILD A *FIRE!*
GAS
S-STILL C-C-COLD!
HOW ABOUT THIS PORTABLE *FURNACE?*
N-N-NOPE! STILL F-F-FREEZING!
IT'S EIGHTY DEGREES AND SUNNY! I'M TOTALLY *SPARKLY!*
GAS
THAT'S NICE. I THINK I B-B-BETTER JUST *CUDDLE* WITH J-BOB. HE'LL KEEP ME W-W-*WARM.*
WELL, OKAY. BUT I KNOW IT'S *FRED* YOU REALLY LOVE. SO THIS WILL BE TOTALLY *TOTALLY* PLATONIC!
I *AM* STILL IN THE TENT, YOU KNOW!
WA-*HOOOO!*
GAS

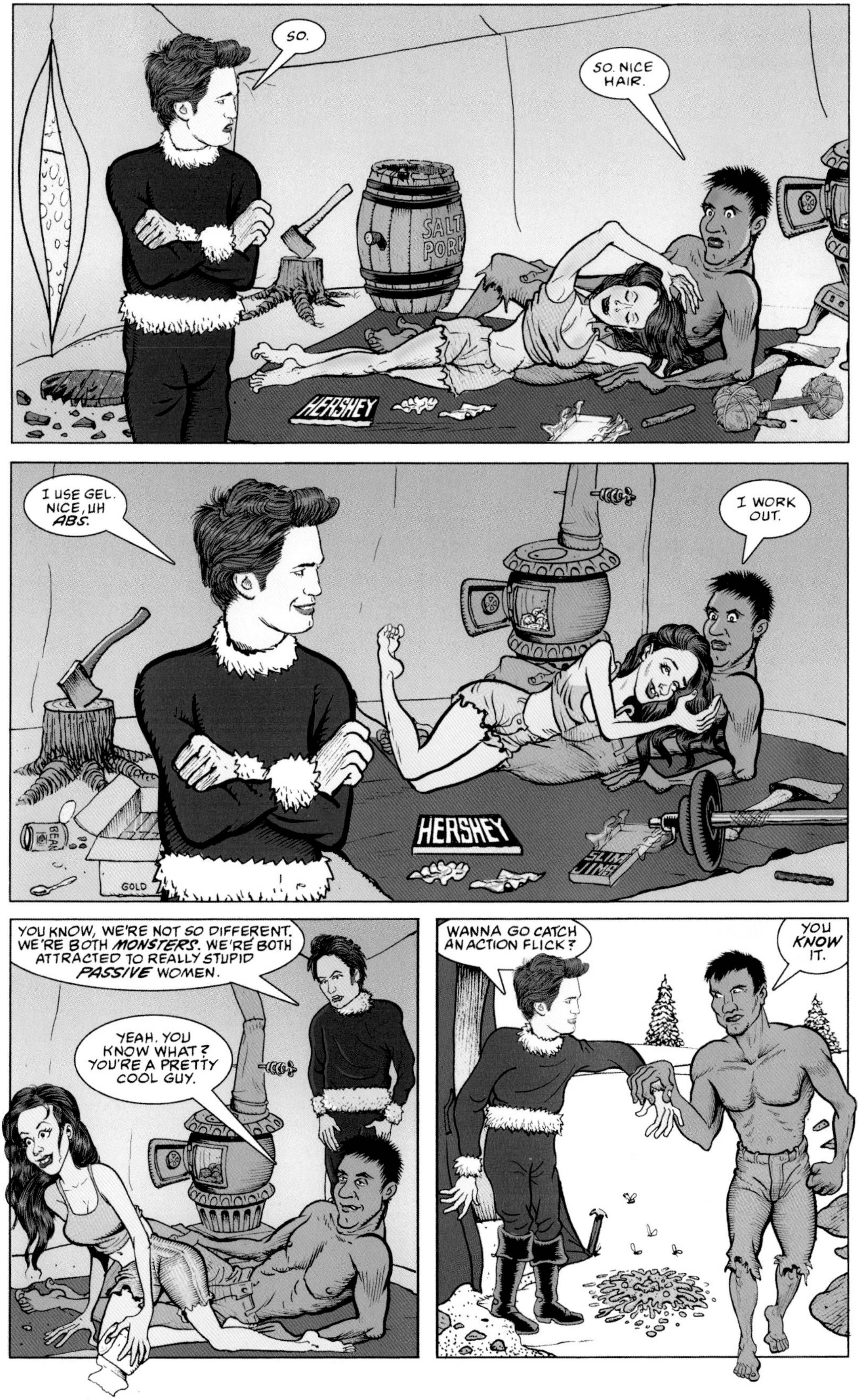
SO.
SO. NICE HAIR.
SALT PORK
HERSHEY
I USE GEL. NICE, UH *ABS*.
I WORK OUT.
HERSHEY
GOLD
YOU KNOW, WE'RE NOT SO DIFFERENT. WE'RE BOTH *MONSTERS*. WE'RE BOTH ATTRACTED TO REALLY STUPID *PASSIVE* WOMEN.
YEAH. YOU KNOW WHAT? YOU'RE A PRETTY COOL GUY.
WANNA GO CATCH AN ACTION FLICK?
YOU *KNOW* IT.

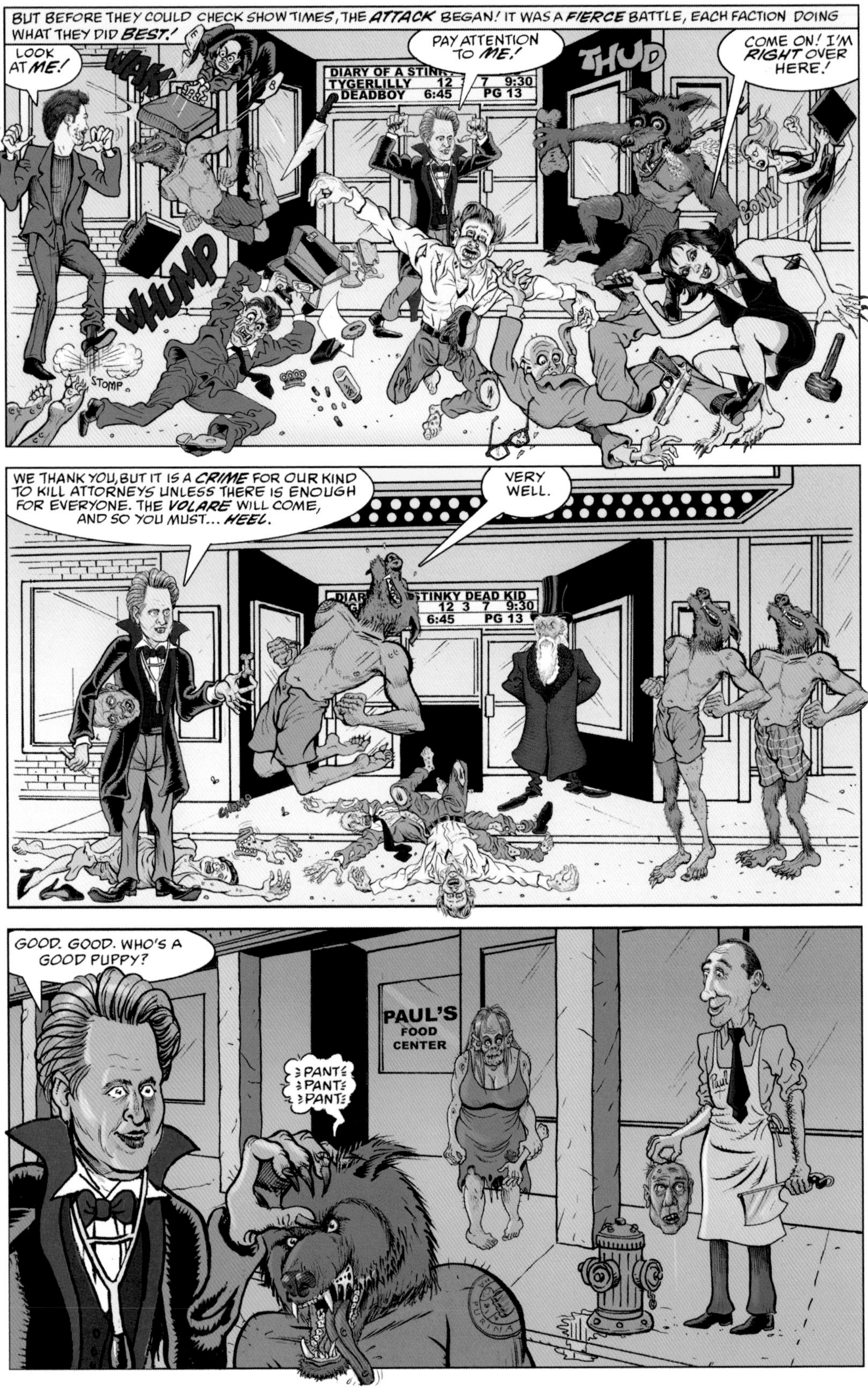
BUT BEFORE THEY COULD CHECK SHOW TIMES, THE ATTACK BEGAN! IT WAS A FIERCE BATTLE, EACH FACTION DOING WHAT THEY DID BEST!
LOOK AT ME!
WAK
PAY ATTENTION TO ME!
DIARY OF A STINK
TYGERLILLY 12 3 7 9:30
DEADBOY 6:45 PG 13
THUD
COME ON! I'M RIGHT OVER HERE!
BONK
WHUMP
STOMP
WE THANK YOU, BUT IT IS A CRIME FOR OUR KIND TO KILL ATTORNEYS UNLESS THERE IS ENOUGH FOR EVERYONE. THE VOLARE WILL COME, AND SO YOU MUST... HEEL.
VERY WELL.
STINKY DEAD KID
12 3 7 9:30
6:45 PG 13
GOOD. GOOD. WHO'S A GOOD PUPPY?
PAUL'S FOOD CENTER
PANT PANT PANT
Paul
PURINA

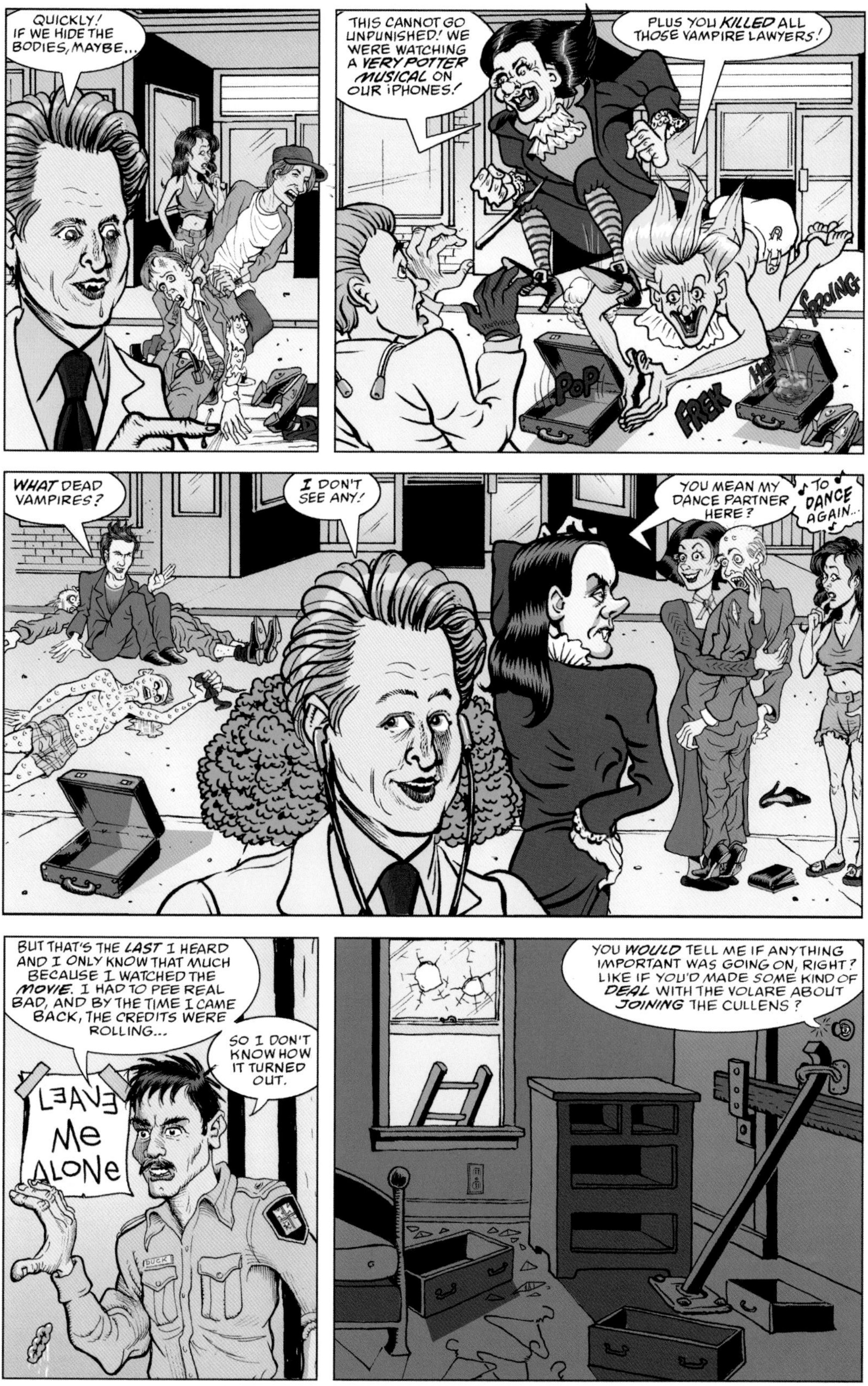
QUICKLY! IF WE HIDE THE BODIES, MAYBE...
THIS CANNOT GO UNPUNISHED! WE WERE WATCHING A VERY POTTER MUSICAL ON OUR iPHONES!
PLUS YOU KILLED ALL THOSE VAMPIRE LAWYERS!
POP
HOP
FREK
SPROING
WHAT DEAD VAMPIRES?
I DON'T SEE ANY!
YOU MEAN MY DANCE PARTNER HERE?
♪ TO DANCE AGAIN... ♪
BUT THAT'S THE LAST I HEARD AND I ONLY KNOW THAT MUCH BECAUSE I WATCHED THE MOVIE. I HAD TO PEE REAL BAD, AND BY THE TIME I CAME BACK, THE CREDITS WERE ROLLING...
SO I DON'T KNOW HOW IT TURNED OUT.
LEAVE ME ALONE
YOU WOULD TELL ME IF ANYTHING IMPORTANT WAS GOING ON, RIGHT? LIKE IF YOU'D MADE SOME KIND OF DEAL WITH THE VOLARE ABOUT JOINING THE CULLENS?

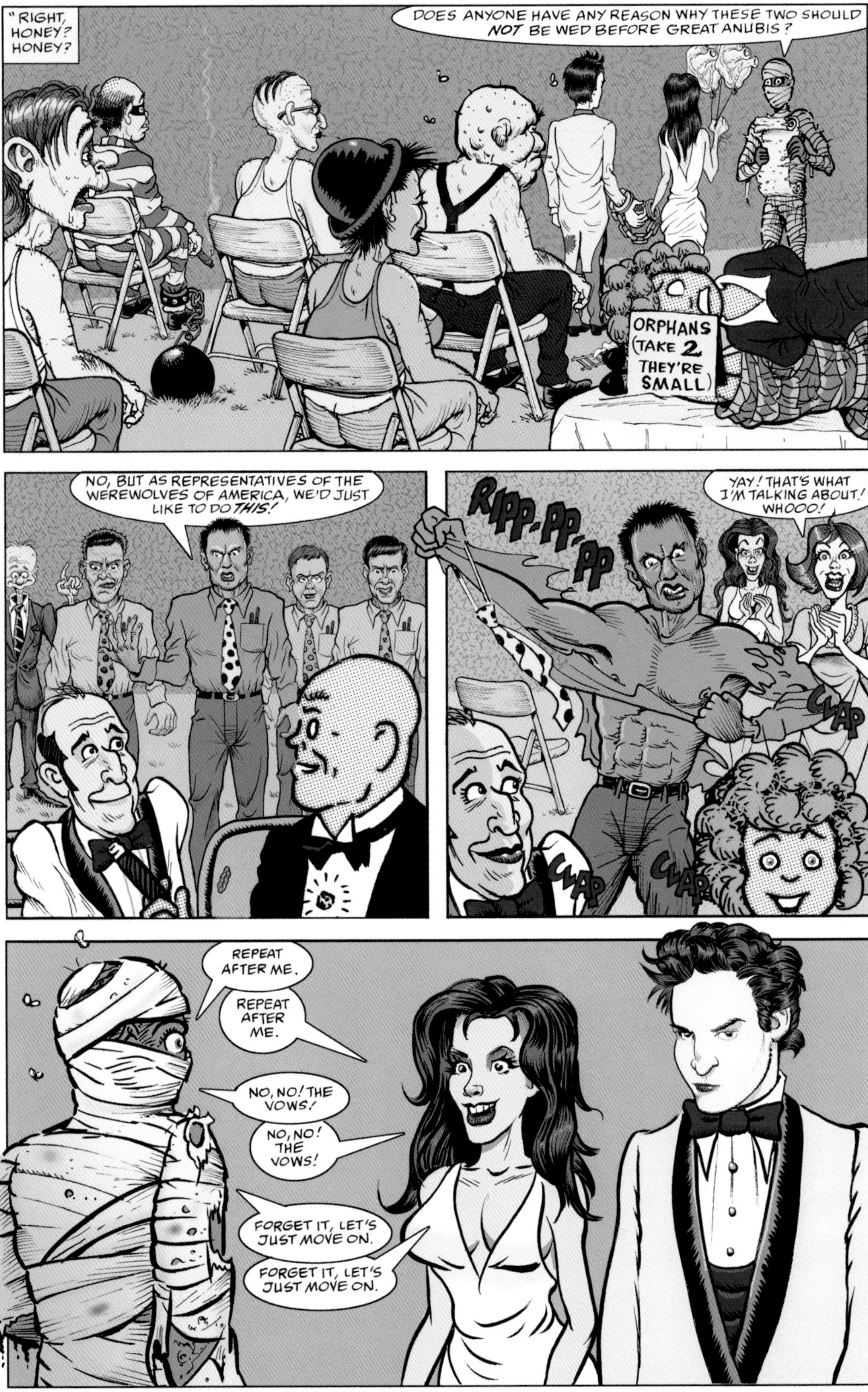

"RIGHT, HONEY? HONEY?
DOES ANYONE HAVE ANY REASON WHY THESE TWO SHOULD *NOT* BE WED BEFORE GREAT ANUBIS?
ORPHANS (TAKE 2 THEY'RE SMALL)
NO, BUT AS REPRESENTATIVES OF THE WEREWOLVES OF AMERICA, WE'D JUST LIKE TO DO *THIS!*
RIPP-PP-PP
YAY! THAT'S WHAT I'M TALKING ABOUT! WHOOO!
CWAP
CWAP
CWAP
REPEAT AFTER ME.
REPEAT AFTER ME.
NO, NO! THE VOWS!
NO, NO! THE VOWS!
FORGET IT, LET'S JUST MOVE ON.
FORGET IT, LET'S JUST MOVE ON.

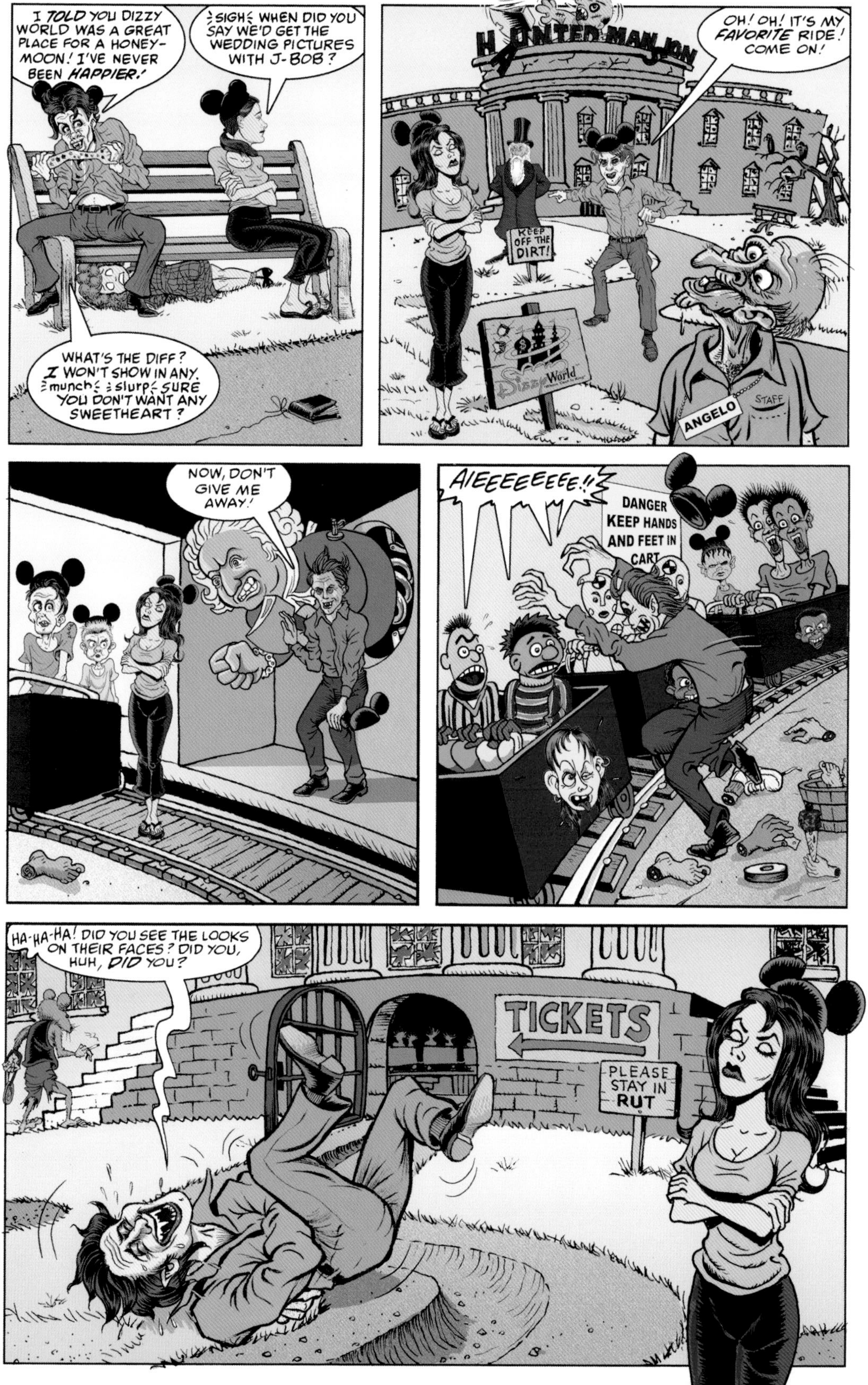
I TOLD YOU DIZZY WORLD WAS A GREAT PLACE FOR A HONEY-MOON! I'VE NEVER BEEN HAPPIER!
SIGH WHEN DID YOU SAY WE'D GET THE WEDDING PICTURES WITH J-BOB?
WHAT'S THE DIFF? I WON'T SHOW IN ANY. munch slurp SURE YOU DON'T WANT ANY SWEETHEART?
HAUNTED MANSION
OH! OH! IT'S MY FAVORITE RIDE! COME ON!
KEEP OFF THE DIRT!
Dizzy World
ANGELO
STAFF
NOW, DON'T GIVE ME AWAY!
AIEEEEEEEE!!
DANGER KEEP HANDS AND FEET IN CART
HA-HA-HA! DID YOU SEE THE LOOKS ON THEIR FACES? DID YOU, HUH, DID YOU?
TICKETS
PLEASE STAY IN RUT

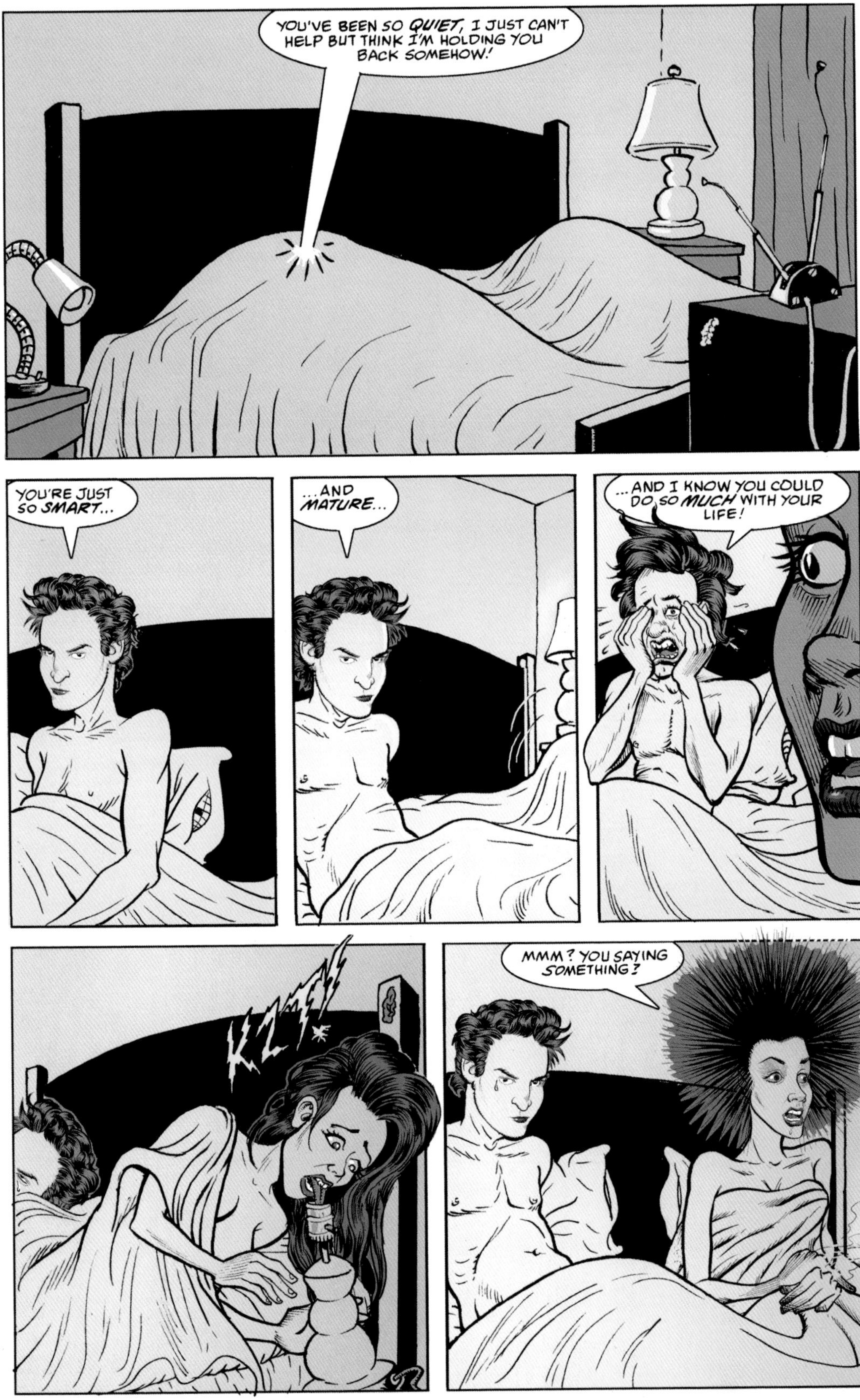
YOU'VE BEEN SO QUIET, I JUST CAN'T HELP BUT THINK I'M HOLDING YOU BACK SOMEHOW!
YOU'RE JUST SO SMART...
...AND MATURE...
...AND I KNOW YOU COULD DO SO MUCH WITH YOUR LIFE!
KZZT!
MMM? YOU SAYING SOMETHING?

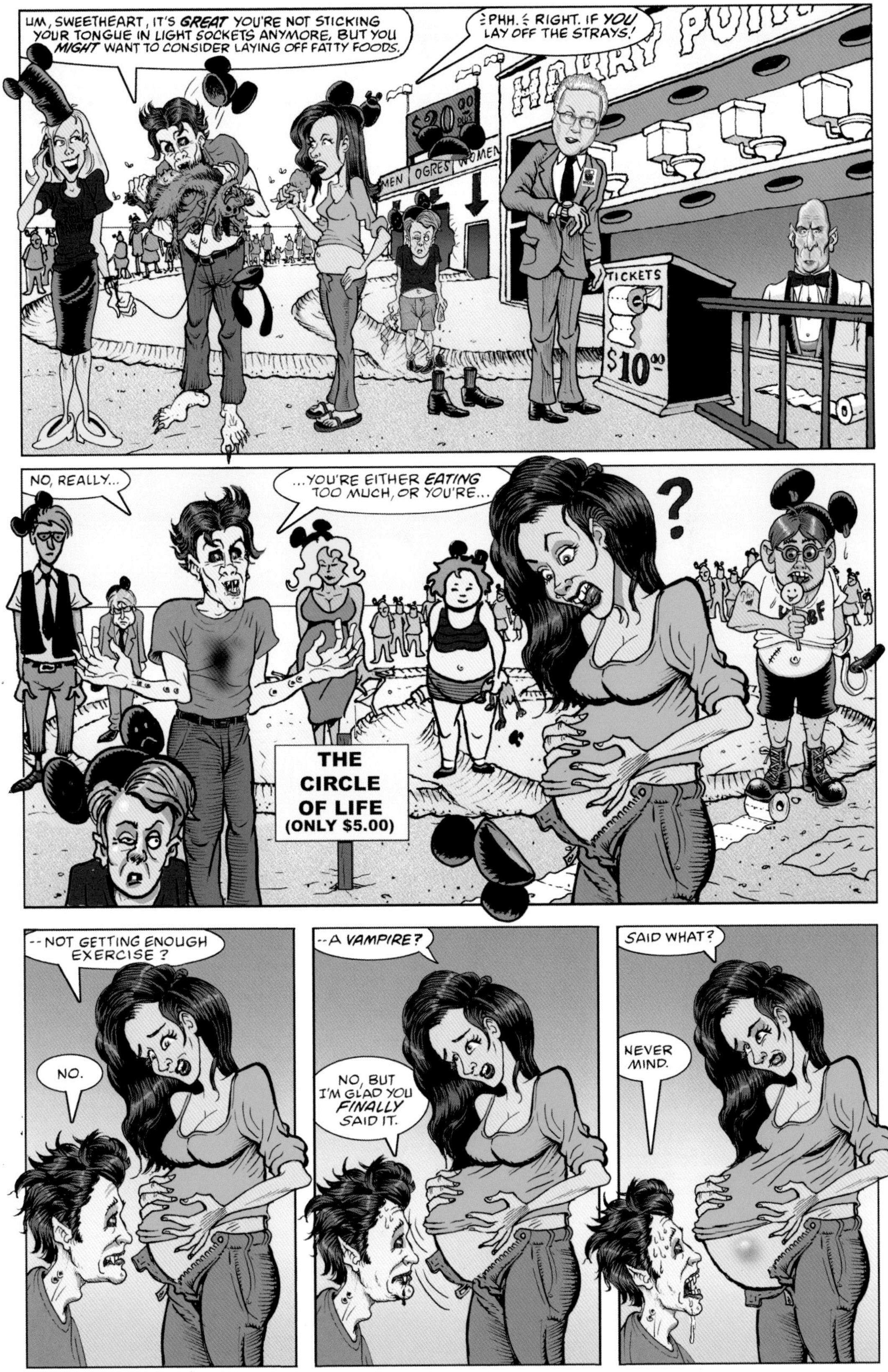
UM, SWEETHEART, IT'S GREAT YOU'RE NOT STICKING YOUR TONGUE IN LIGHT SOCKETS ANYMORE, BUT YOU MIGHT WANT TO CONSIDER LAYING OFF FATTY FOODS.
PHH. RIGHT. IF YOU LAY OFF THE STRAYS!
HARRY POTT
$20.00
MEN OGRES WOMEN
TICKETS
$10.00
NO, REALLY...
...YOU'RE EITHER EATING TOO MUCH, OR YOU'RE...
?
THE CIRCLE OF LIFE (ONLY $5.00)
--NOT GETTING ENOUGH EXERCISE?
NO.
--A VAMPIRE?
NO, BUT I'M GLAD YOU FINALLY SAID IT.
SAID WHAT?
NEVER MIND.

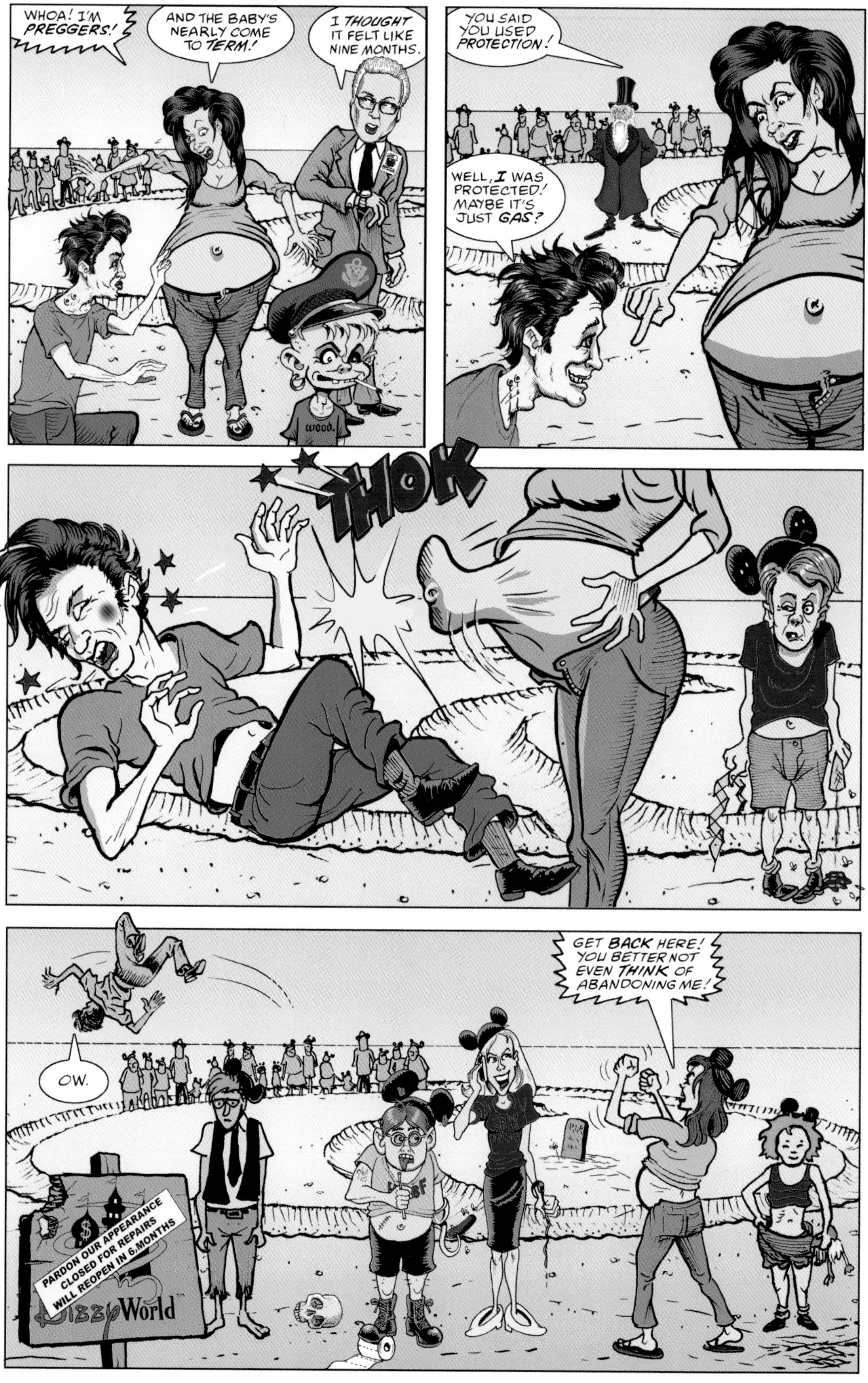

WHOA! I'M PREGGERS!
AND THE BABY'S NEARLY COME TO TERM!
I THOUGHT IT FELT LIKE NINE MONTHS.
wood.
YOU SAID YOU USED PROTECTION!
WELL, I WAS PROTECTED! MAYBE IT'S JUST GAS?
THOK
GET BACK HERE! YOU BETTER NOT EVEN THINK OF ABANDONING ME!
OW.
PARDON OUR APPEARANCE
CLOSED FOR REPAIRS
WILL REOPEN IN 6 MONTHS
Dizzy World™

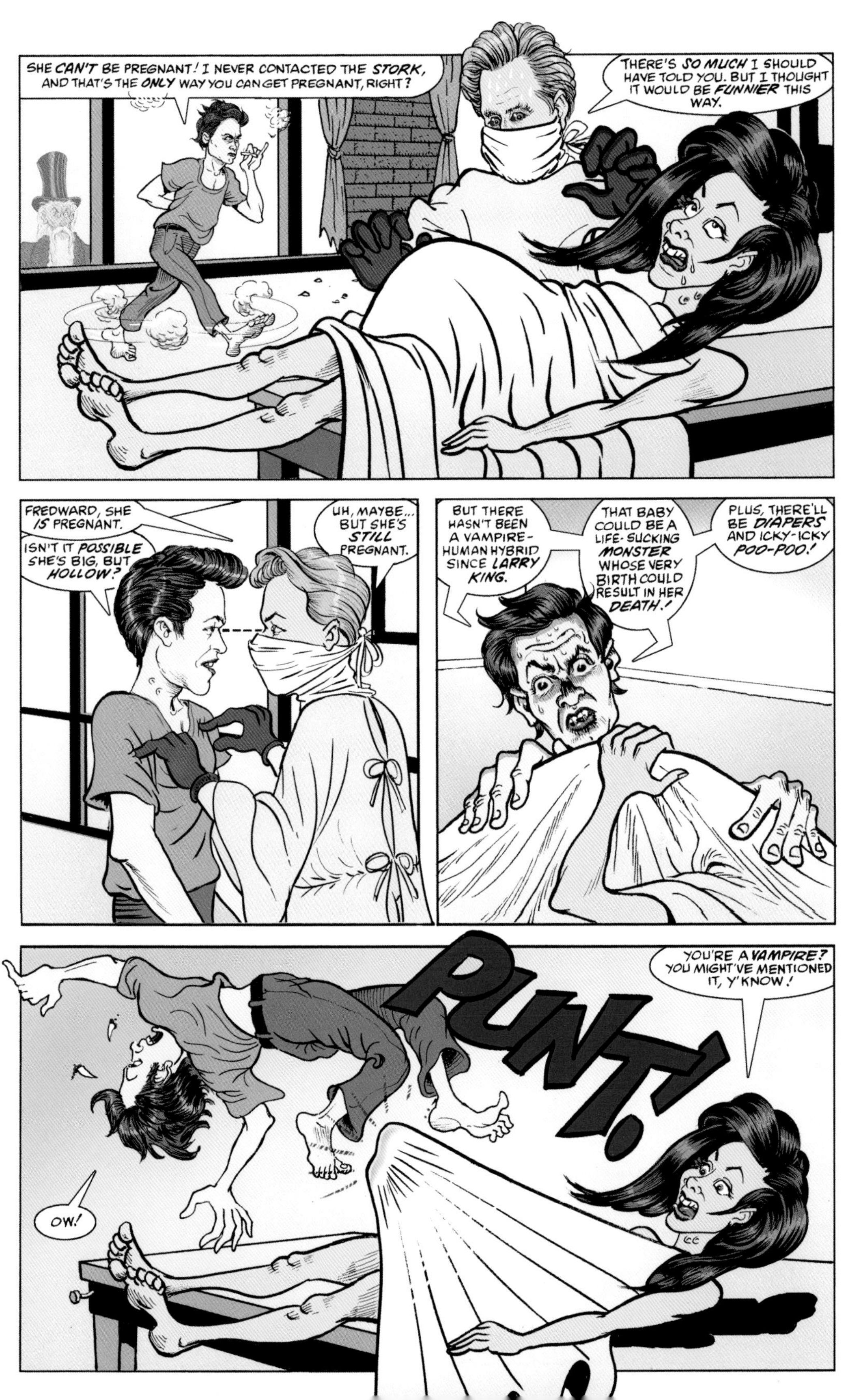
SHE CAN'T BE PREGNANT! I NEVER CONTACTED THE STORK, AND THAT'S THE ONLY WAY YOU CAN GET PREGNANT, RIGHT?
THERE'S SO MUCH I SHOULD HAVE TOLD YOU. BUT I THOUGHT IT WOULD BE FUNNIER THIS WAY.
FREDWARD, SHE IS PREGNANT.
ISN'T IT POSSIBLE SHE'S BIG, BUT HOLLOW?
UH, MAYBE... BUT SHE'S STILL PREGNANT.
BUT THERE HASN'T BEEN A VAMPIRE-HUMAN HYBRID SINCE LARRY KING.
THAT BABY COULD BE A LIFE-SUCKING MONSTER WHOSE VERY BIRTH COULD RESULT IN HER DEATH!
PLUS, THERE'LL BE DIAPERS AND ICKY-ICKY POO-POO!
PUNT!
YOU'RE A VAMPIRE? YOU MIGHT'VE MENTIONED IT, Y'KNOW!
OW!

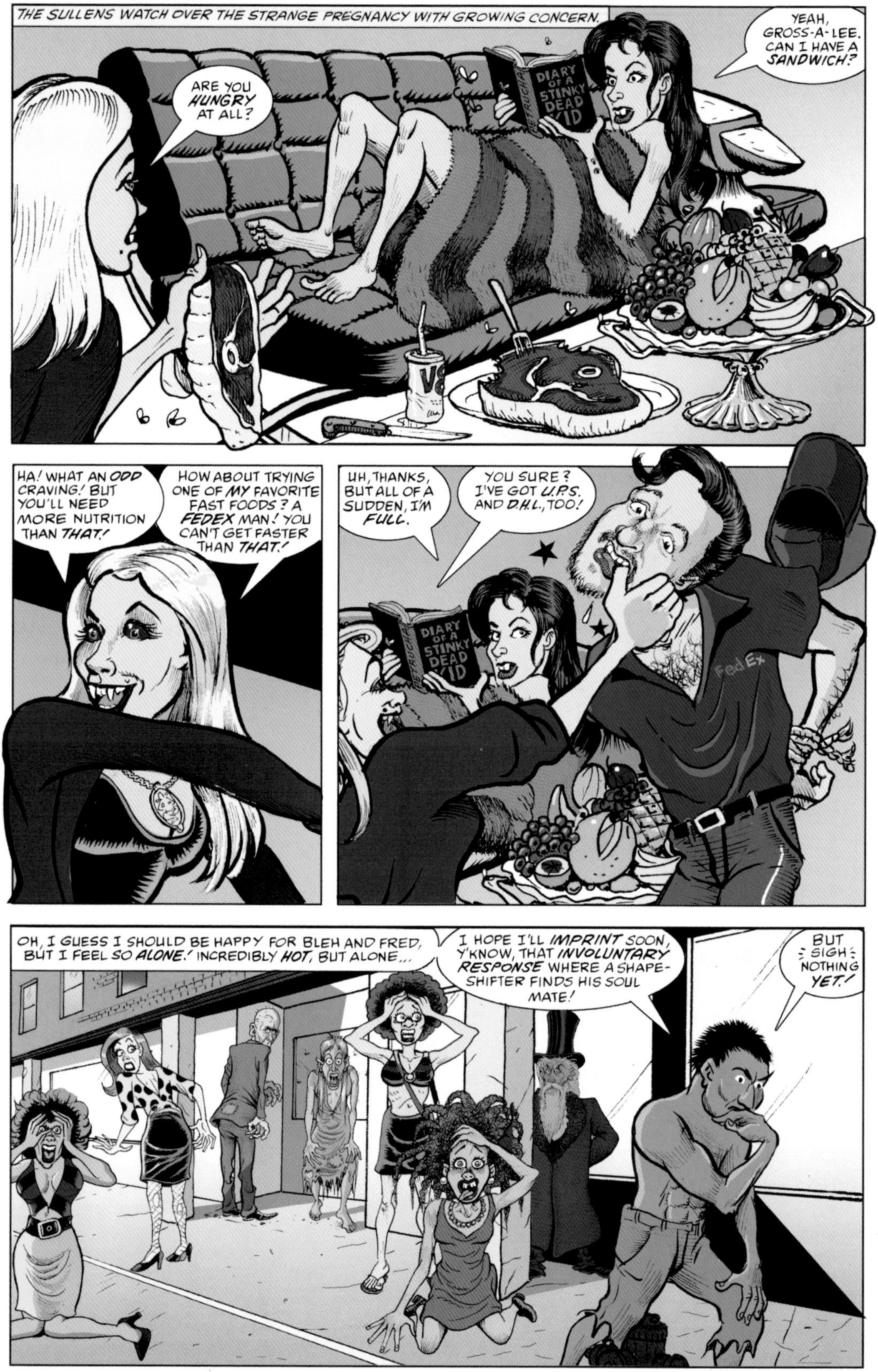
THE SULLENS WATCH OVER THE STRANGE PREGNANCY WITH GROWING CONCERN.
ARE YOU HUNGRY AT ALL?
YEAH, GROSS-A-LEE. CAN I HAVE A SANDWICH?
DIARY OF A STINKY DEAD KID
TRUCCIA
HA! WHAT AN ODD CRAVING! BUT YOU'LL NEED MORE NUTRITION THAN THAT!
HOW ABOUT TRYING ONE OF MY FAVORITE FAST FOODS? A FEDEX MAN! YOU CAN'T GET FASTER THAN THAT!
UH, THANKS, BUT ALL OF A SUDDEN, I'M FULL.
YOU SURE? I'VE GOT U.P.S. AND D.H.L., TOO!
DIARY OF A STINKY DEAD KID
TRUCCIA
FedEx
OH, I GUESS I SHOULD BE HAPPY FOR BLEH AND FRED, BUT I FEEL SO ALONE! INCREDIBLY HOT, BUT ALONE...
I HOPE I'LL IMPRINT SOON, Y'KNOW, THAT INVOLUNTARY RESPONSE WHERE A SHAPE-SHIFTER FINDS HIS SOUL MATE!
BUT SIGH NOTHING YET!

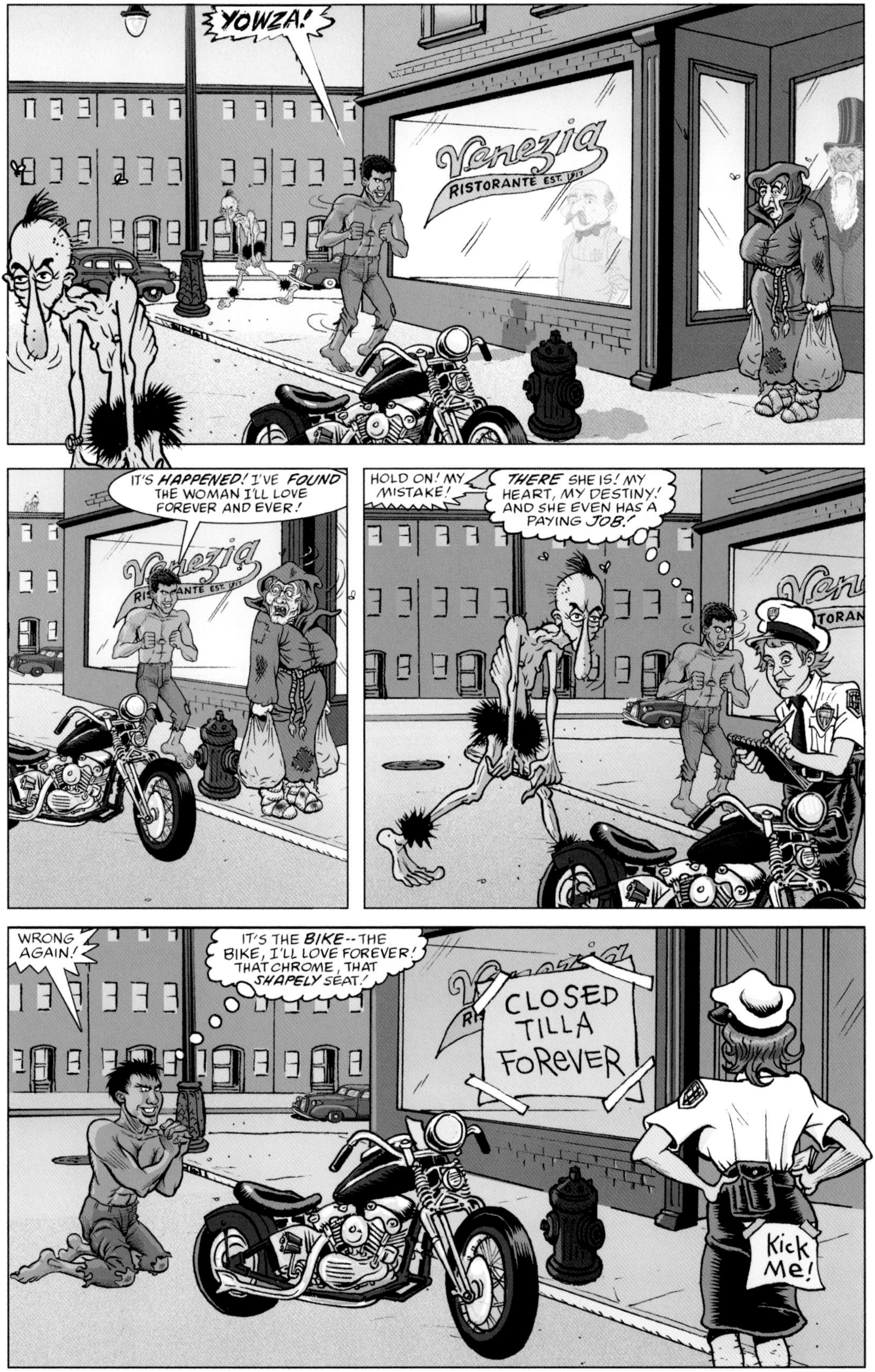
YOWZA!
Venezia
RISTORANTE EST. 1917
IT'S HAPPENED! I'VE FOUND THE WOMAN I'LL LOVE FOREVER AND EVER!
HOLD ON! MY MISTAKE!
THERE SHE IS! MY HEART, MY DESTINY! AND SHE EVEN HAS A PAYING JOB!
WRONG AGAIN!
IT'S THE BIKE-- THE BIKE, I'LL LOVE FOREVER! THAT CHROME, THAT SHAPELY SEAT!
CLOSED TILLA FOREVER
Kick Me!

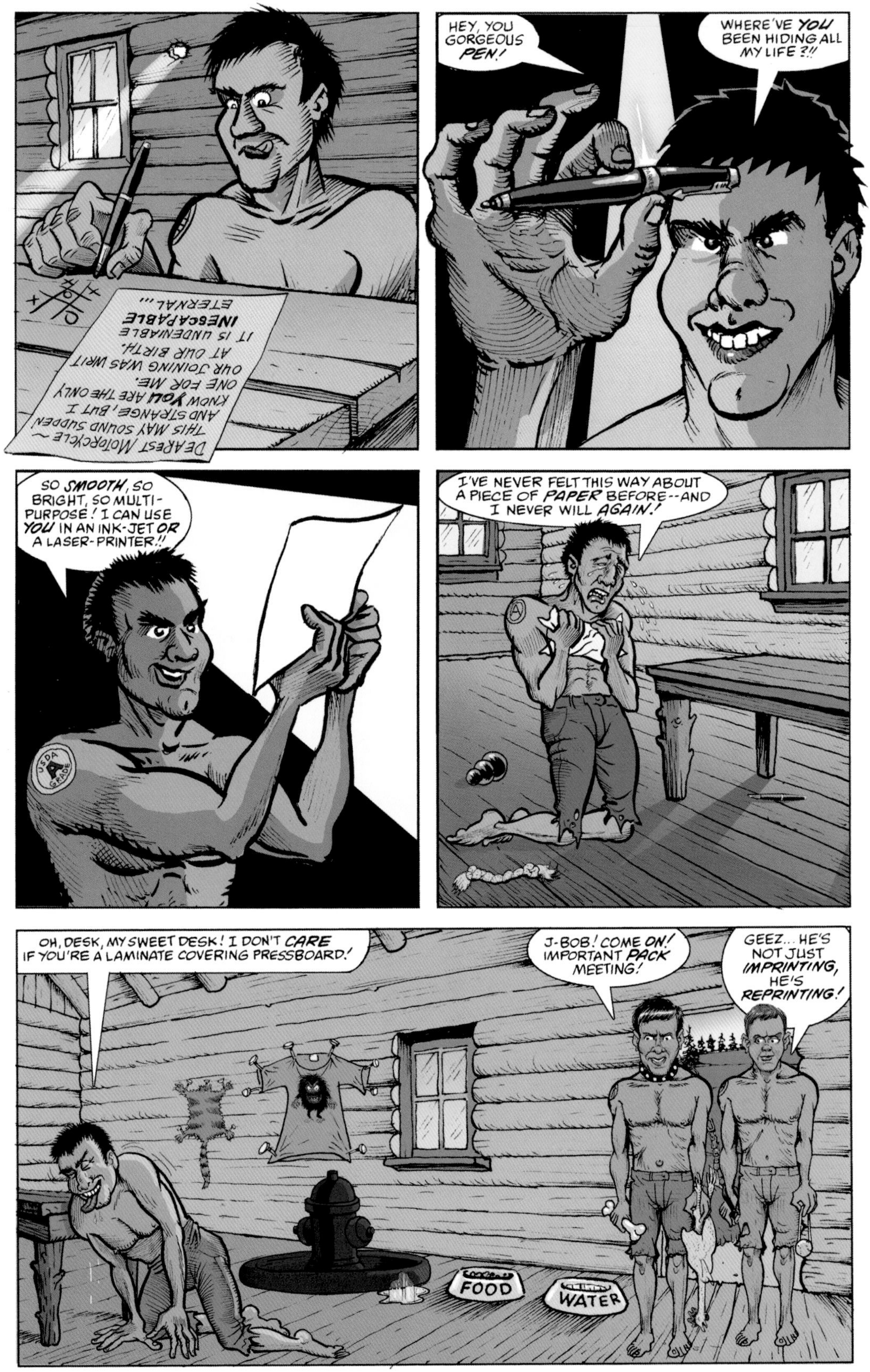

DEAREST MOTORCYCLE ~ THIS MAY SOUND SUDDEN AND STRANGE, BUT I KNOW YOU ARE THE ONLY ONE FOR ME. OUR JOINING WAS WRIT AT OUR BIRTH. IT IS UNDENIABLE INESCAPABLE ETERNAL...
HEY, YOU GORGEOUS PEN!
WHERE'VE YOU BEEN HIDING ALL MY LIFE?!!
SO SMOOTH, SO BRIGHT, SO MULTI-PURPOSE! I CAN USE YOU IN AN INK-JET OR A LASER-PRINTER!!
USDA GRADE
I'VE NEVER FELT THIS WAY ABOUT A PIECE OF PAPER BEFORE--AND I NEVER WILL AGAIN!
OH, DESK, MY SWEET DESK! I DON'T CARE IF YOU'RE A LAMINATE COVERING PRESSBOARD!
J-BOB! COME ON! IMPORTANT PACK MEETING!
GEEZ... HE'S NOT JUST IMPRINTING, HE'S REPRINTING!
FOOD
WATER

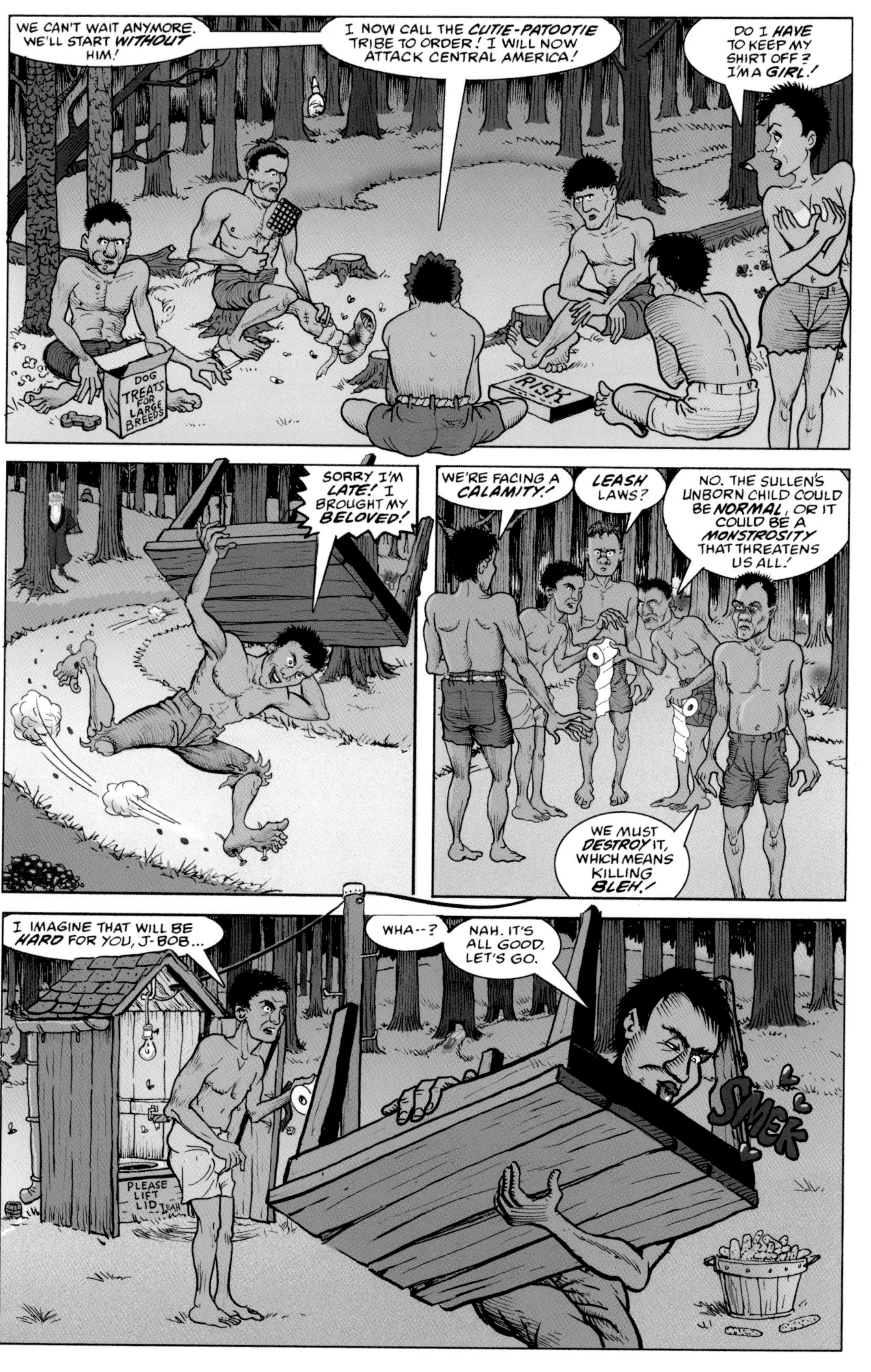

WE CAN'T WAIT ANYMORE. WE'LL START WITHOUT HIM!
I NOW CALL THE CUTIE-PATOOTIE TRIBE TO ORDER! I WILL NOW ATTACK CENTRAL AMERICA!
DO I HAVE TO KEEP MY SHIRT OFF? I'M A GIRL!
DOG TREATS FOR LARGE BREEDS
RISK
SORRY I'M LATE! I BROUGHT MY BELOVED!
WE'RE FACING A CALAMITY!
LEASH LAWS?
NO. THE SULLEN'S UNBORN CHILD COULD BE NORMAL, OR IT COULD BE A MONSTROSITY THAT THREATENS US ALL!
WE MUST DESTROY IT, WHICH MEANS KILLING BLEH!
I IMAGINE THAT WILL BE HARD FOR YOU, J-BOB...
WHA--?
NAH. IT'S ALL GOOD, LET'S GO.
PLEASE LIFT LID —LEAH
SMEK

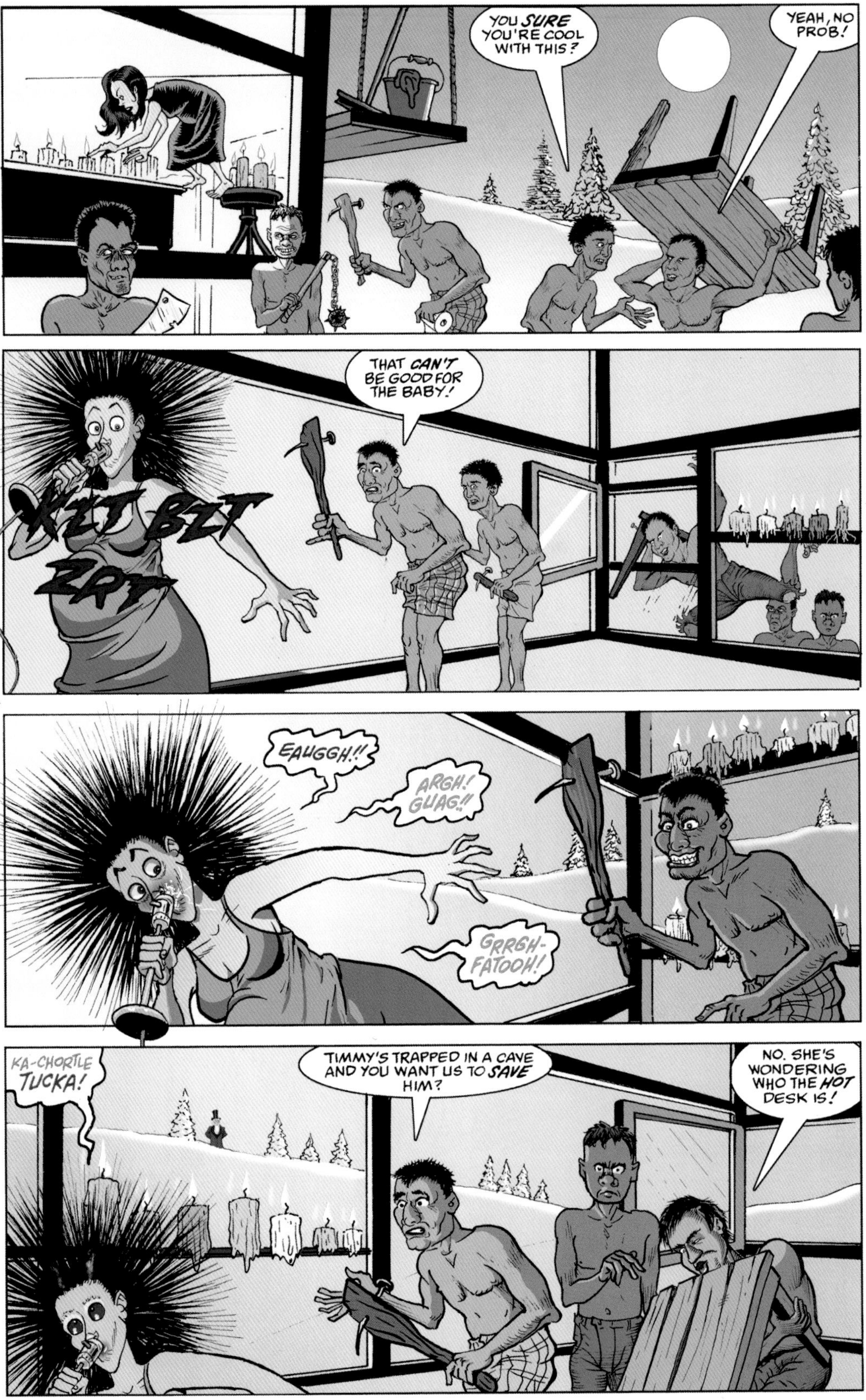
YOU SURE YOU'RE COOL WITH THIS?
YEAH, NO PROB!
THAT CAN'T BE GOOD FOR THE BABY!
BZT BZT ZRT
EAUGGH!!
ARGH! GUAG!!
GRRGH-FATOOH!
KA-CHORTLE TUCKA!
TIMMY'S TRAPPED IN A CAVE AND YOU WANT US TO SAVE HIM?
NO. SHE'S WONDERING WHO THE HOT DESK IS!

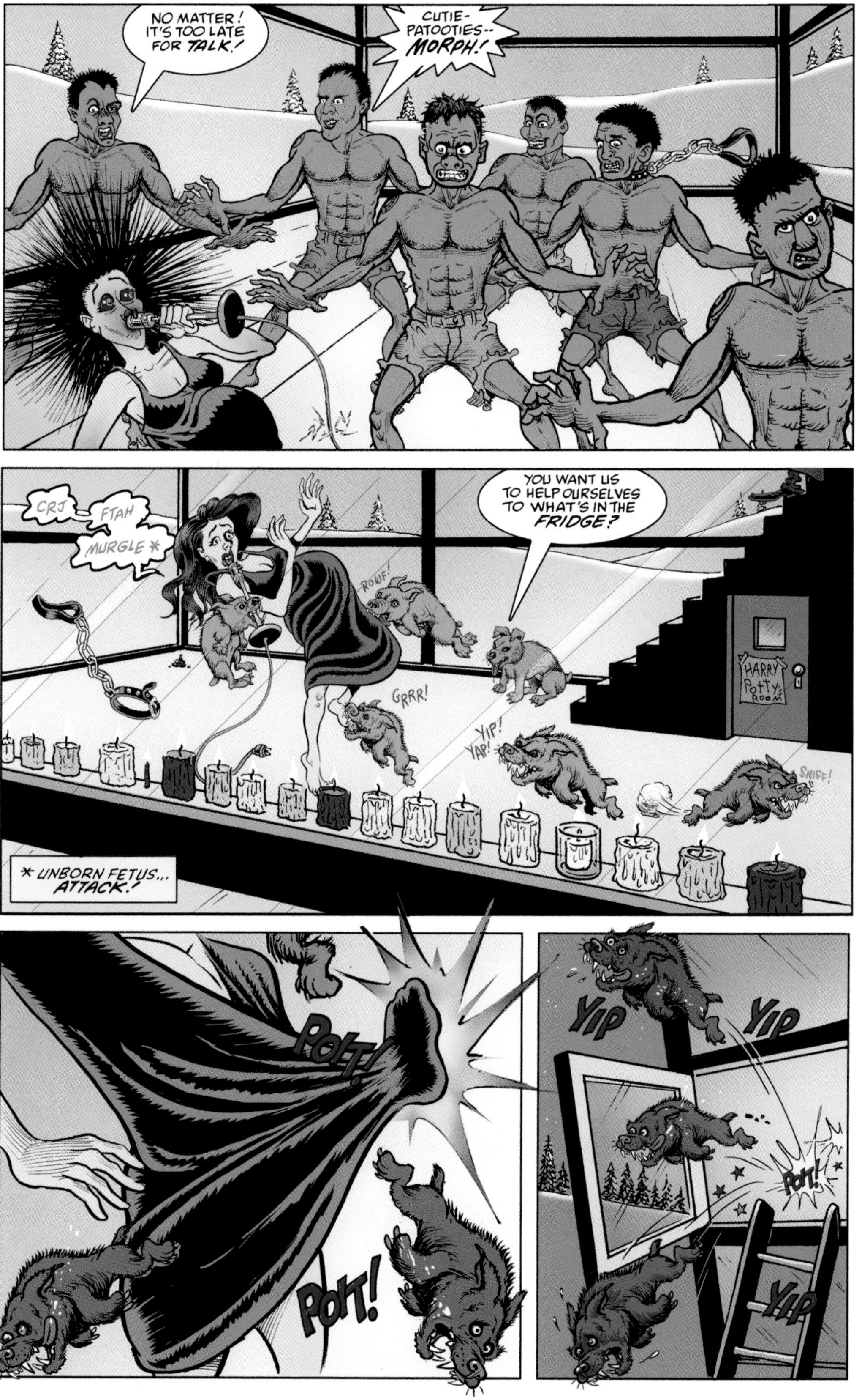
NO MATTER! IT'S TOO LATE FOR TALK!
CUTIE-PATOOTIES-- MORPH!
CRJ
FTAH
MURGLE *
ROWF!
YOU WANT US TO HELP OURSELVES TO WHAT'S IN THE FRIDGE?
HARRY POTTY'S ROOM
GRRR!
YIP! YAP!
SNIFF!
* UNBORN FETUS... ATTACK!
POIT!
POIT!
YIP
YIP
POIT!
YIP

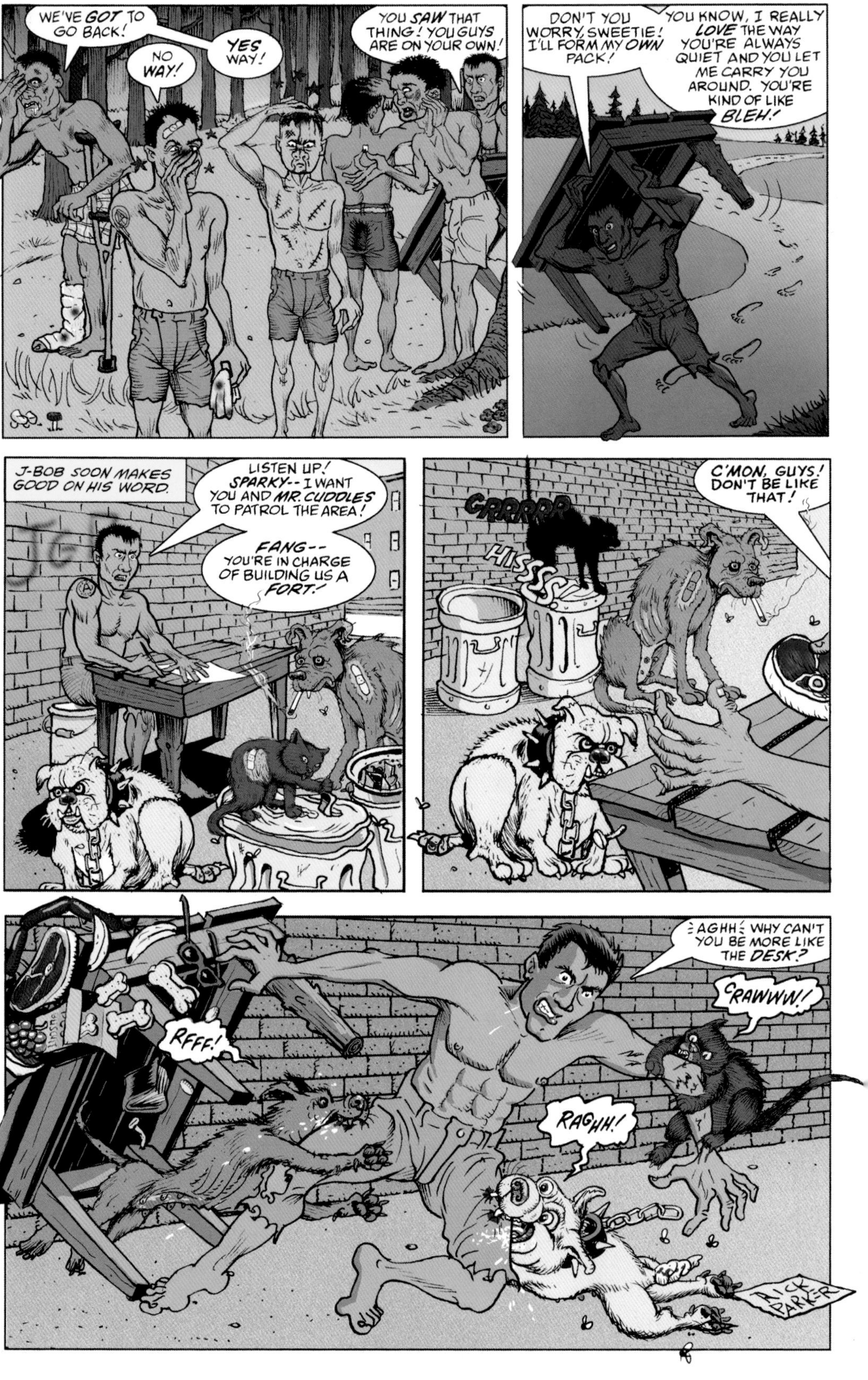

WE'VE GOT TO GO BACK!
NO WAY!
YES WAY!
YOU SAW THAT THING! YOU GUYS ARE ON YOUR OWN!
DON'T YOU WORRY, SWEETIE! I'LL FORM MY OWN PACK!
YOU KNOW, I REALLY LOVE THE WAY YOU'RE ALWAYS QUIET AND YOU LET ME CARRY YOU AROUND. YOU'RE KIND OF LIKE BLEH!
J-BOB SOON MAKES GOOD ON HIS WORD.
LISTEN UP! SPARKY-- I WANT YOU AND MR. CUDDLES TO PATROL THE AREA!
FANG-- YOU'RE IN CHARGE OF BUILDING US A FORT!
GRRRRR
HISSSS!
C'MON, GUYS! DON'T BE LIKE THAT!
AGHH! WHY CAN'T YOU BE MORE LIKE THE DESK?
CRAWWW!
RFFF!
RAGHH!
RICK PARKER

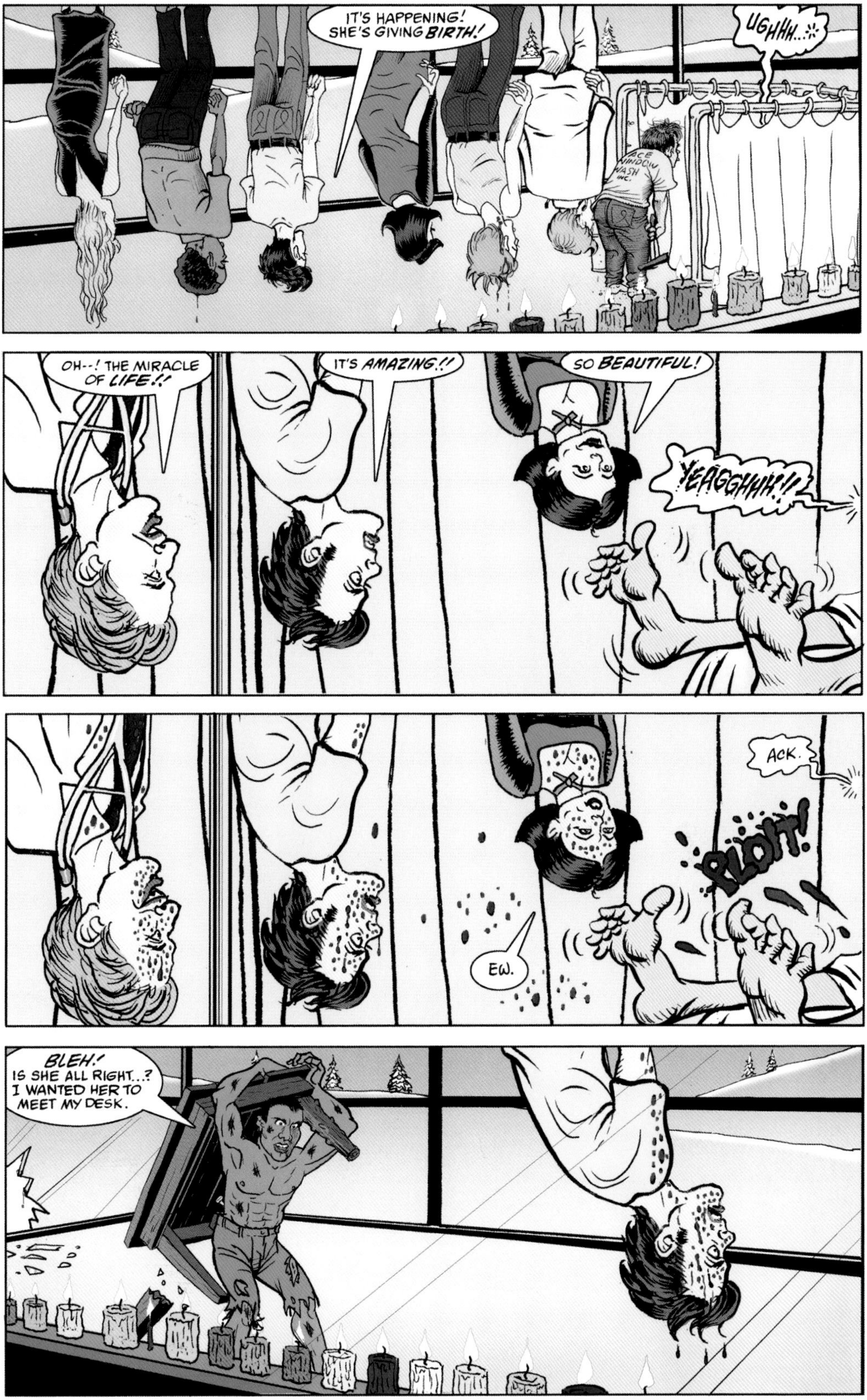
IT'S HAPPENING! SHE'S GIVING BIRTH!
UGHHH...
ACE WINDOW WASH INC.
OH--! THE MIRACLE OF LIFE!!
IT'S AMAZING!!
SO BEAUTIFUL!
YEAGGHHH!!
ACK.
PLOIT!
EW.
BLEH! IS SHE ALL RIGHT...? I WANTED HER TO MEET MY DESK.

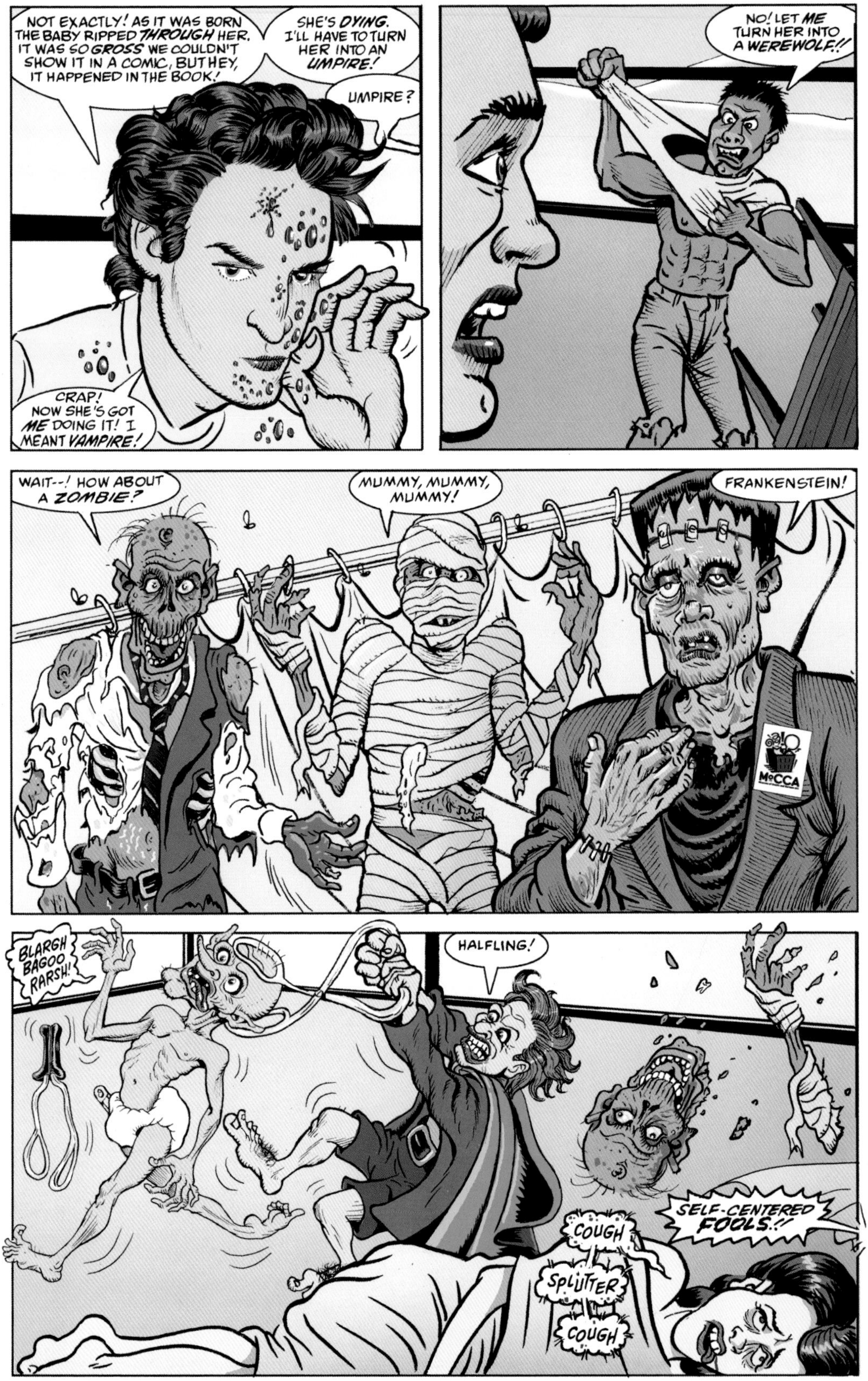
NOT EXACTLY! AS IT WAS BORN THE BABY RIPPED THROUGH HER. IT WAS SO GROSS WE COULDN'T SHOW IT IN A COMIC, BUT HEY, IT HAPPENED IN THE BOOK!
SHE'S DYING. I'LL HAVE TO TURN HER INTO AN UMPIRE!
UMPIRE?
CRAP! NOW SHE'S GOT ME DOING IT! I MEANT VAMPIRE!
NO! LET ME TURN HER INTO A WEREWOLF!!
WAIT--! HOW ABOUT A ZOMBIE?
MUMMY, MUMMY, MUMMY!
FRANKENSTEIN!
MoCCA
BLARGH BAGOO RARSH!
HALFLING!
SELF-CENTERED FOOLS!!
COUGH
SPLUTTER
COUGH

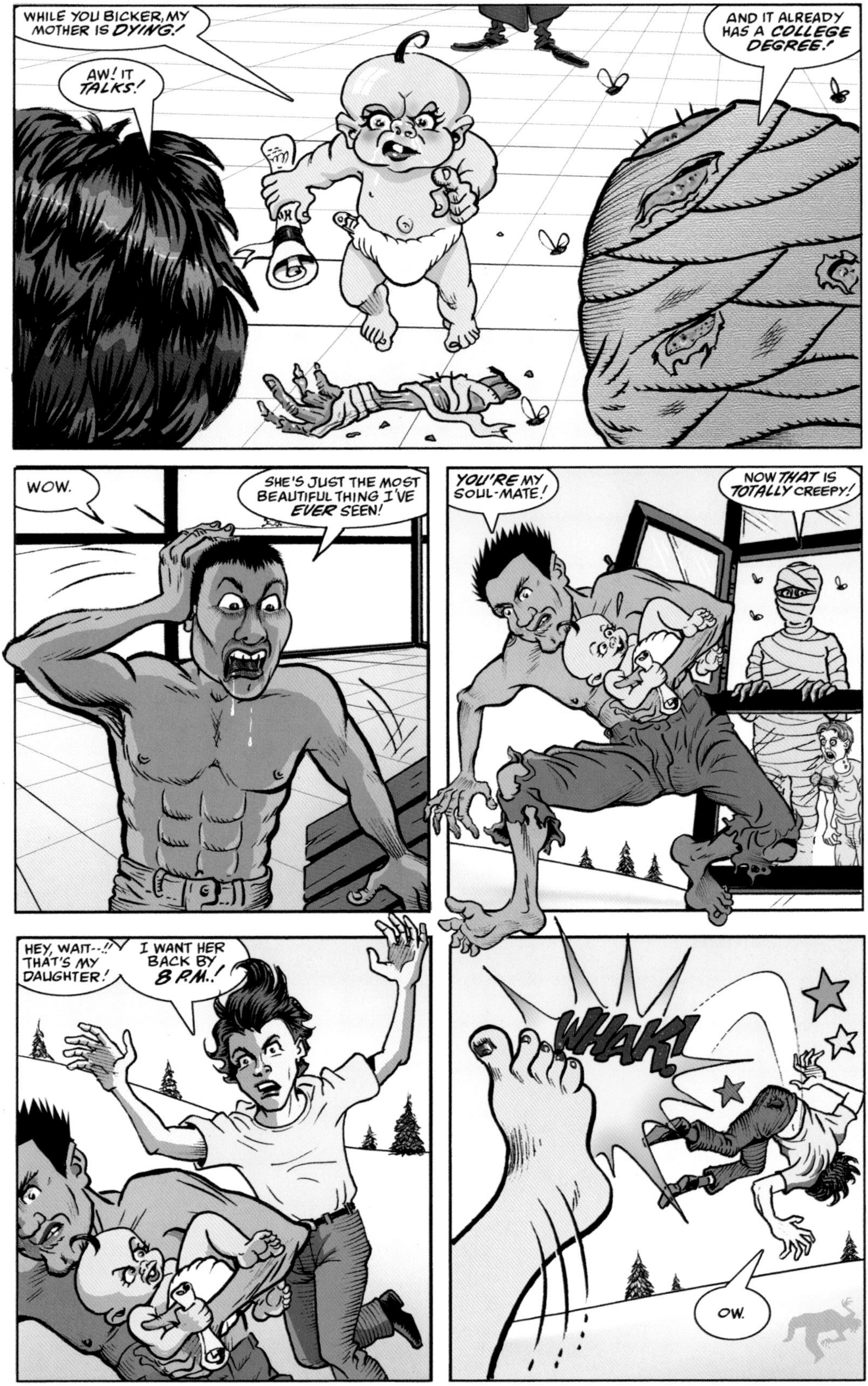
WHILE YOU BICKER, MY MOTHER IS *DYING!*
AW! IT *TALKS!*
AND IT ALREADY HAS A *COLLEGE DEGREE!*
WOW.
SHE'S JUST THE MOST BEAUTIFUL THING I'VE *EVER* SEEN!
YOU'RE MY SOUL-MATE!
NOW *THAT* IS *TOTALLY* CREEPY!
HEY, WAIT--!! THAT'S MY DAUGHTER!
I WANT HER BACK BY *8 P.M.!*
WHAK!
OW.

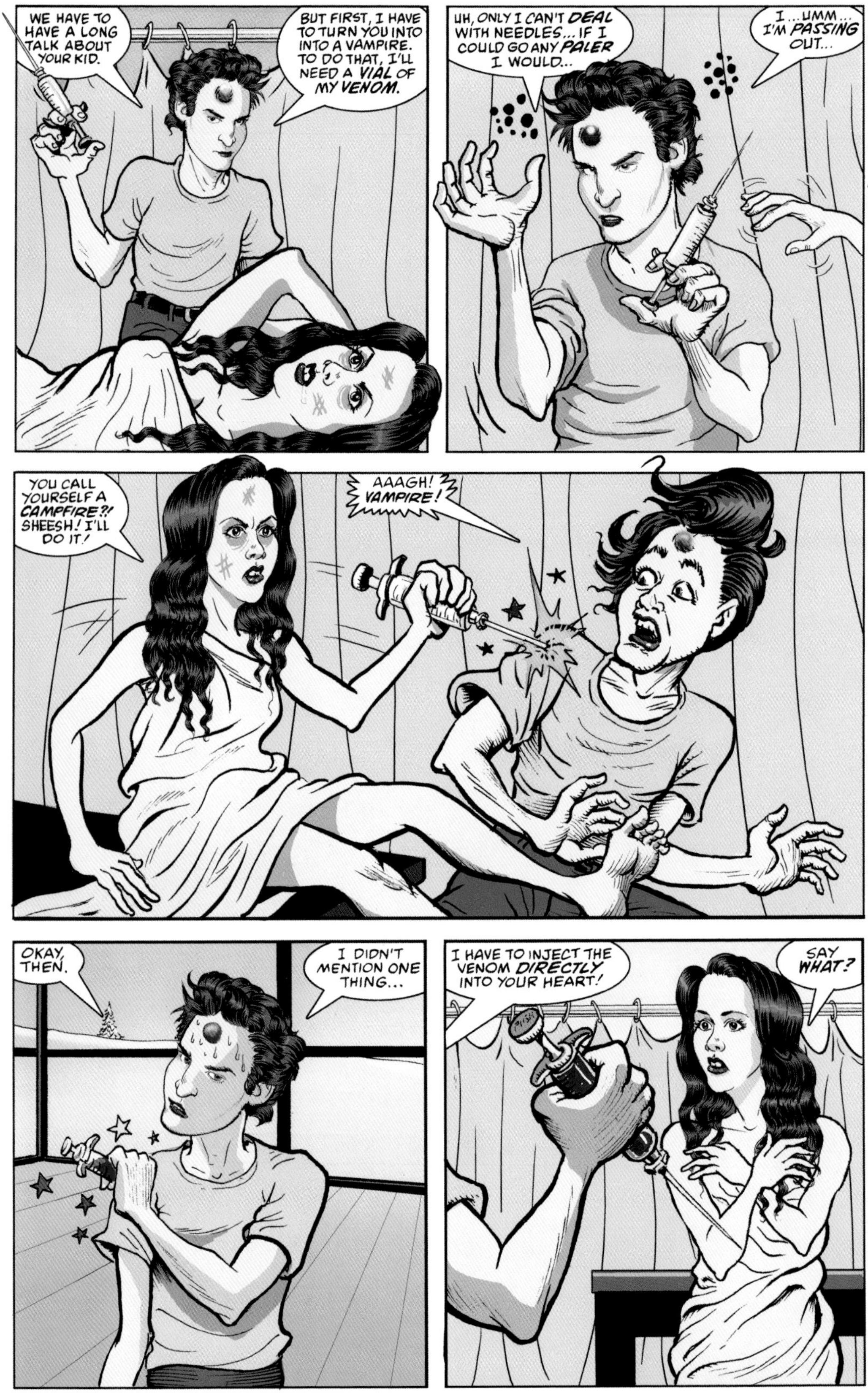

WE HAVE TO HAVE A LONG TALK ABOUT YOUR KID.
BUT FIRST, I HAVE TO TURN YOU INTO INTO A VAMPIRE. TO DO THAT, I'LL NEED A VIAL OF MY VENOM.
UH, ONLY I CAN'T DEAL WITH NEEDLES... IF I COULD GO ANY PALER I WOULD...
I...UMM... I'M PASSING OUT...
YOU CALL YOURSELF A CAMPFIRE?! SHEESH! I'LL DO IT!
AAAGH! VAMPIRE!
OKAY, THEN.
I DIDN'T MENTION ONE THING...
I HAVE TO INJECT THE VENOM DIRECTLY INTO YOUR HEART!
SAY WHAT?

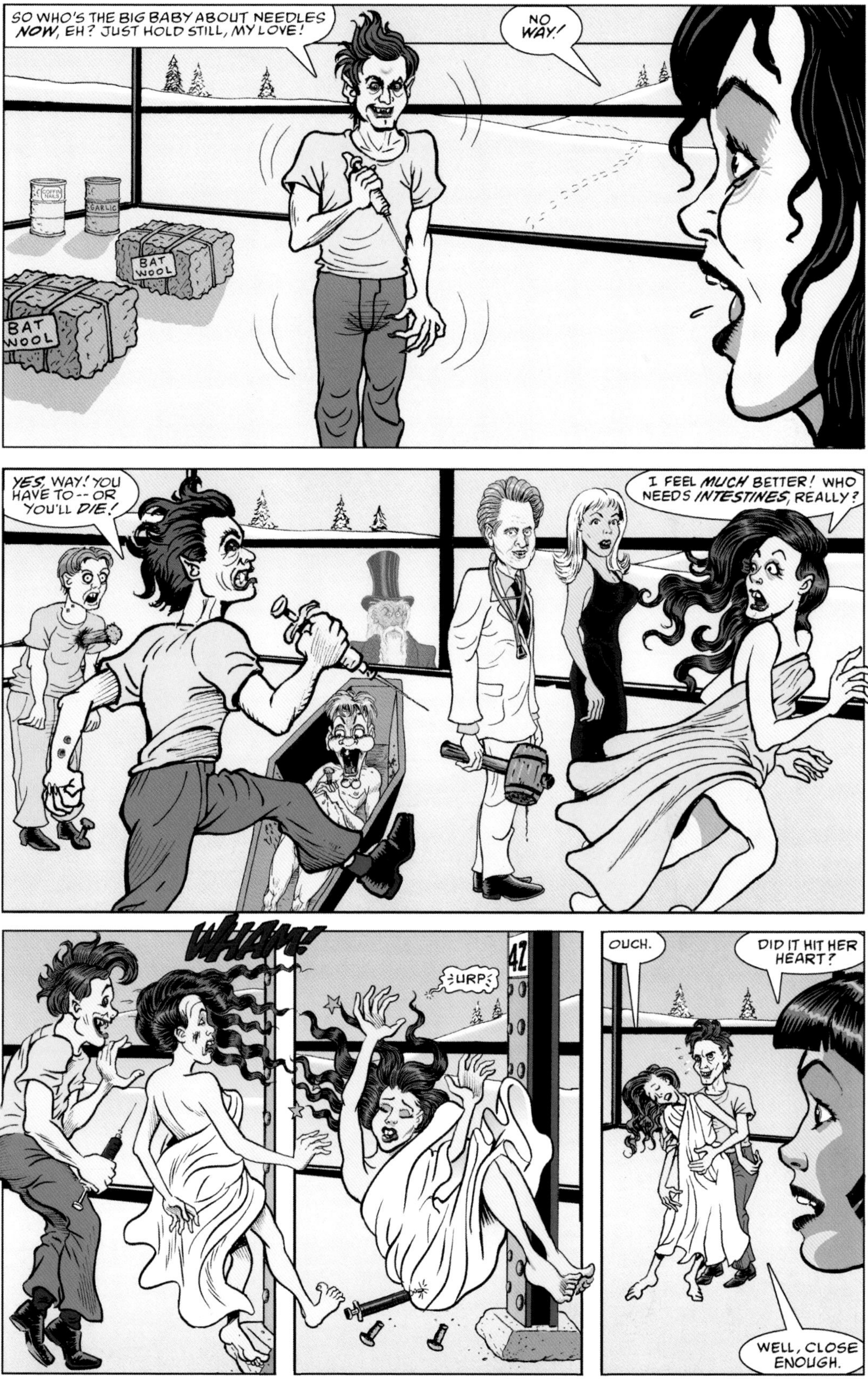
SO WHO'S THE BIG BABY ABOUT NEEDLES NOW, EH? JUST HOLD STILL, MY LOVE!
NO WAY!
COFFIN NAILS
GARLIC
BAT WOOL
BAT WOOL
YES, WAY! YOU HAVE TO -- OR YOU'LL DIE!
I FEEL MUCH BETTER! WHO NEEDS INTESTINES, REALLY?
WHAM!
URP
42
OUCH.
DID IT HIT HER HEART?
WELL, CLOSE ENOUGH.

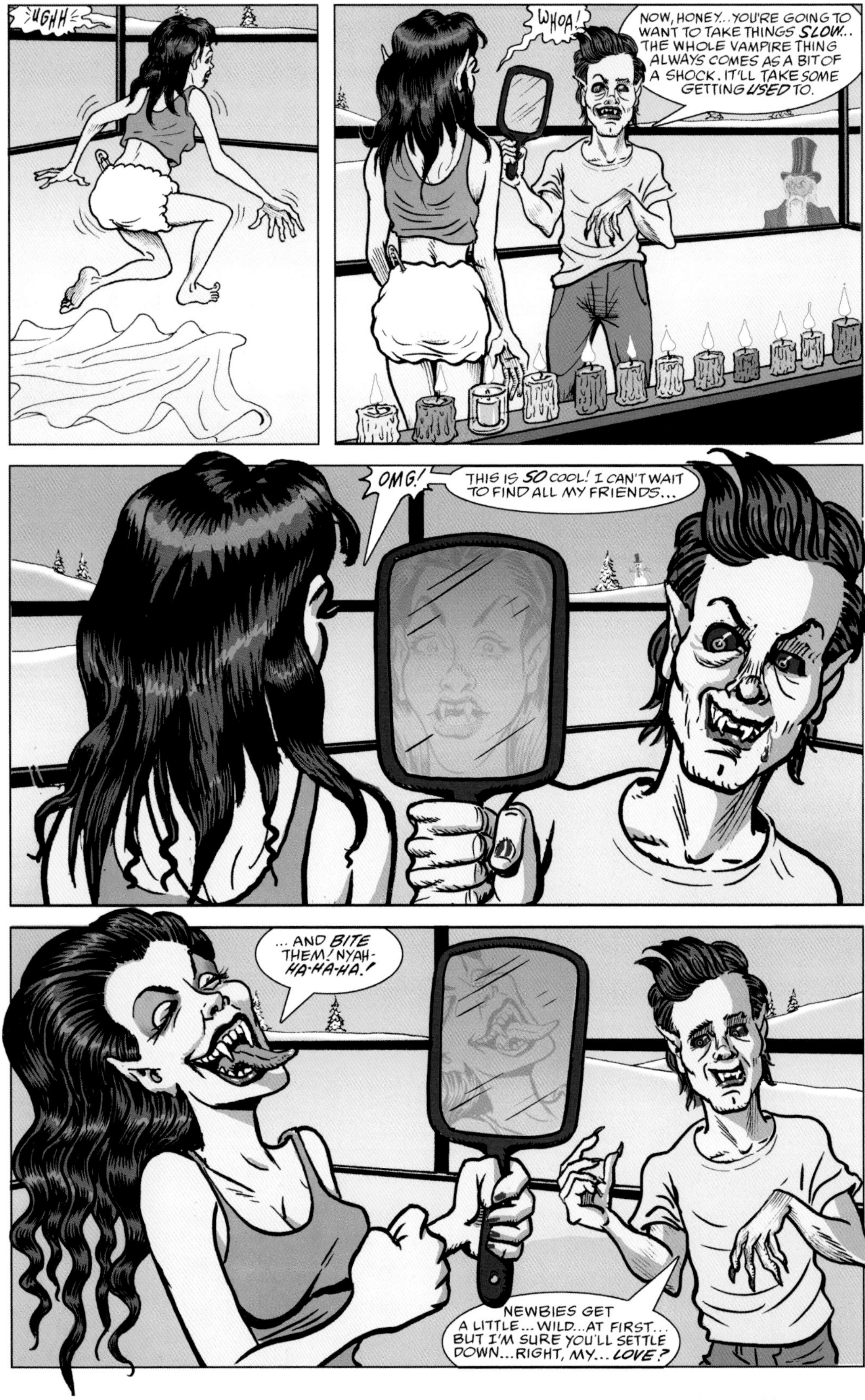
UGHH
WHOA!
NOW, HONEY... YOU'RE GOING TO WANT TO TAKE THINGS SLOW... THE WHOLE VAMPIRE THING ALWAYS COMES AS A BIT OF A SHOCK. IT'LL TAKE SOME GETTING USED TO.
OMG!
THIS IS SO COOL! I CAN'T WAIT TO FIND ALL MY FRIENDS...
... AND BITE THEM! NYAH-HA-HA-HA!
NEWBIES GET A LITTLE... WILD... AT FIRST... BUT I'M SURE YOU'LL SETTLE DOWN... RIGHT, MY... LOVE?

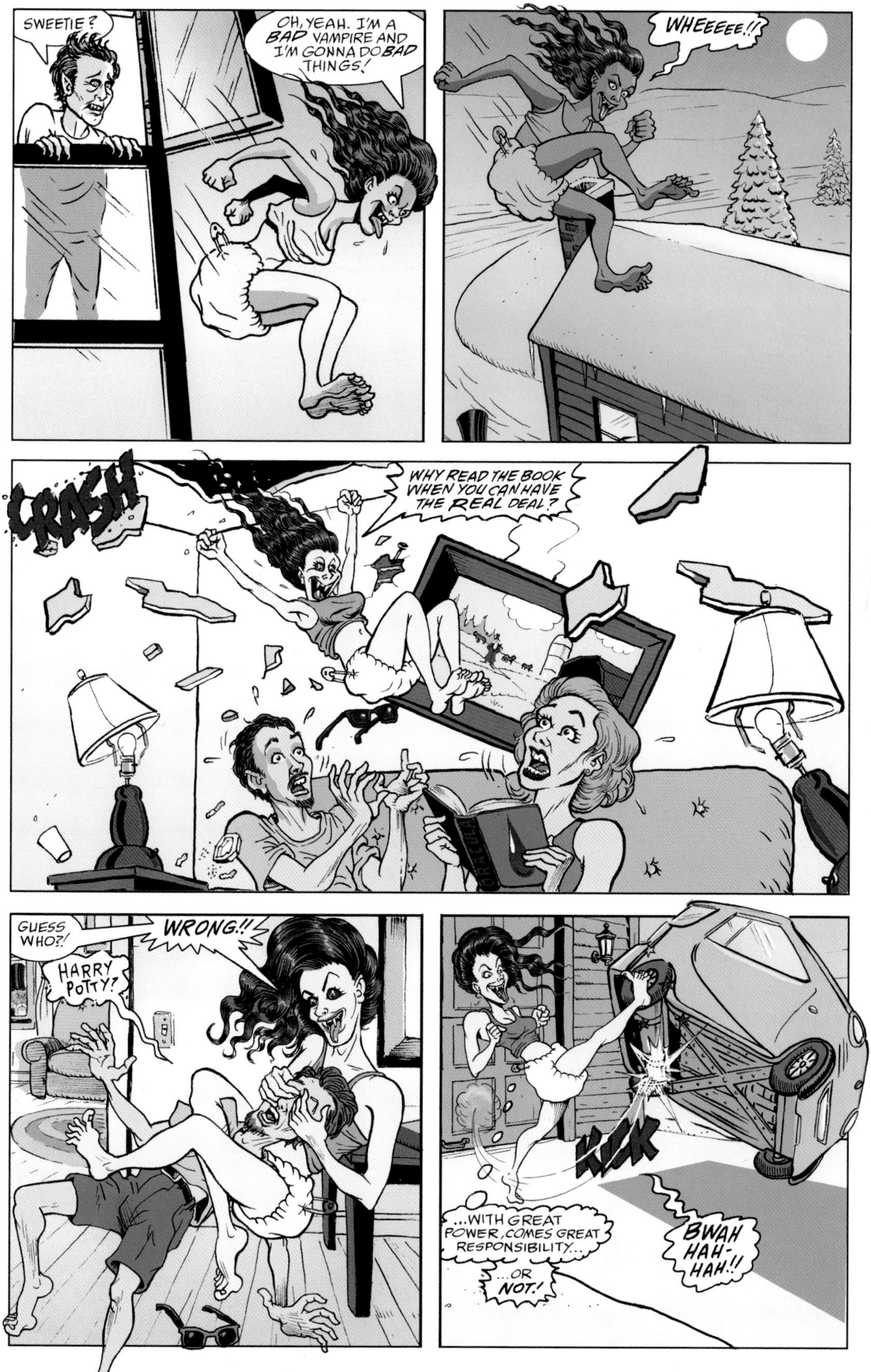
SWEETIE?
OH, YEAH. I'M A BAD VAMPIRE AND I'M GONNA DO BAD THINGS!
WHEEEEEE!!
CRASH
WHY READ THE BOOK WHEN YOU CAN HAVE THE REAL DEAL?
DRACULA
GUESS WHO?!
WRONG!!
HARRY POTTY?
KICK
...WITH GREAT POWER, COMES GREAT RESPONSIBILITY...
...OR NOT!
BWAH HAH HAH!!

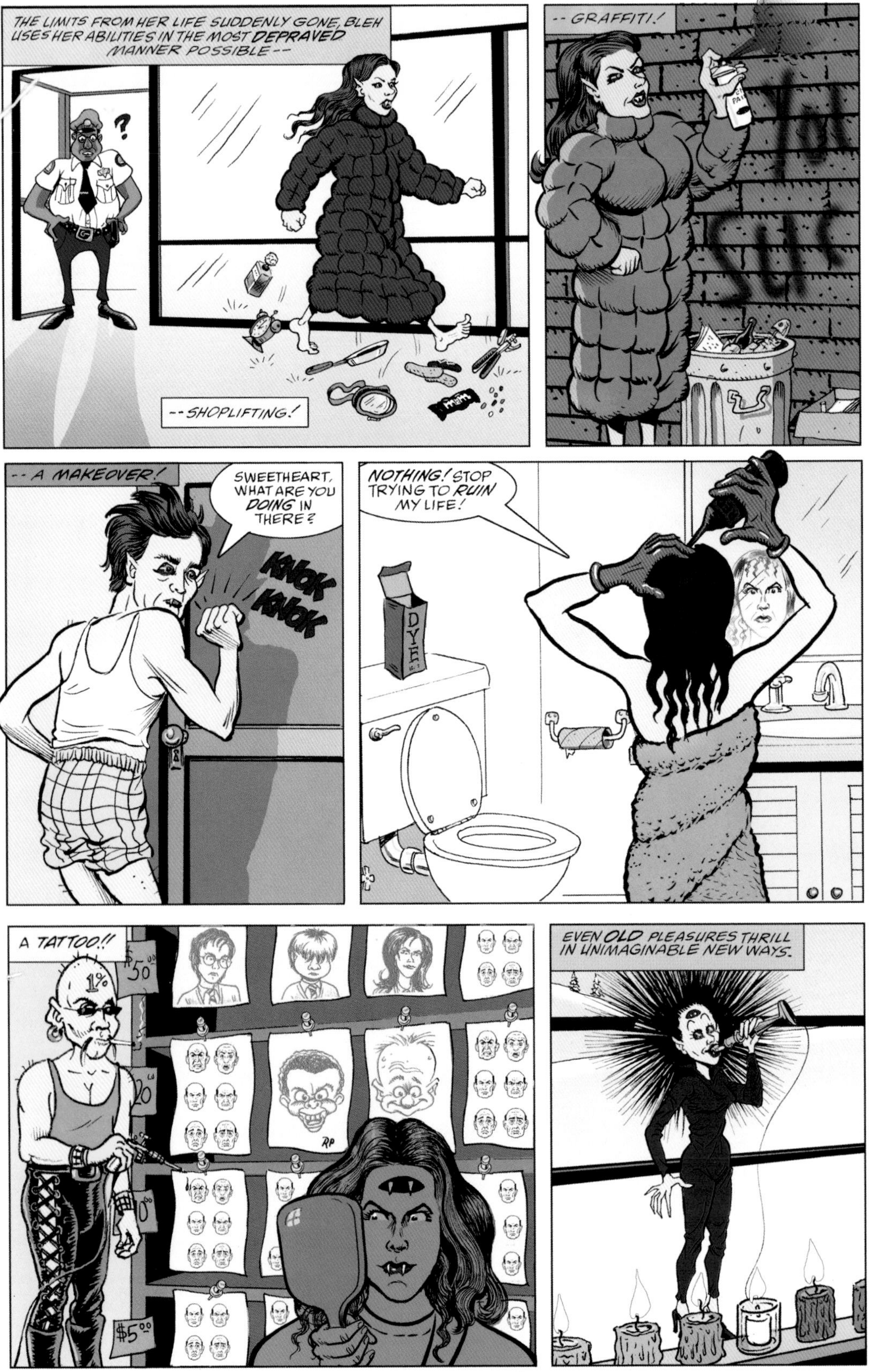
THE LIMITS FROM HER LIFE SUDDENLY GONE, BLEH USES HER ABILITIES IN THE MOST DEPRAVED MANNER POSSIBLE--
?
--SHOPLIFTING!
--GRAFFITI!
--A MAKEOVER!
SWEETHEART, WHAT ARE YOU DOING IN THERE?
KNOK KNOK
NOTHING! STOP TRYING TO RUIN MY LIFE!
DYE
A TATTOO!!
$50.00
$5.00
EVEN OLD PLEASURES THRILL IN UNIMAGINABLE NEW WAYS.

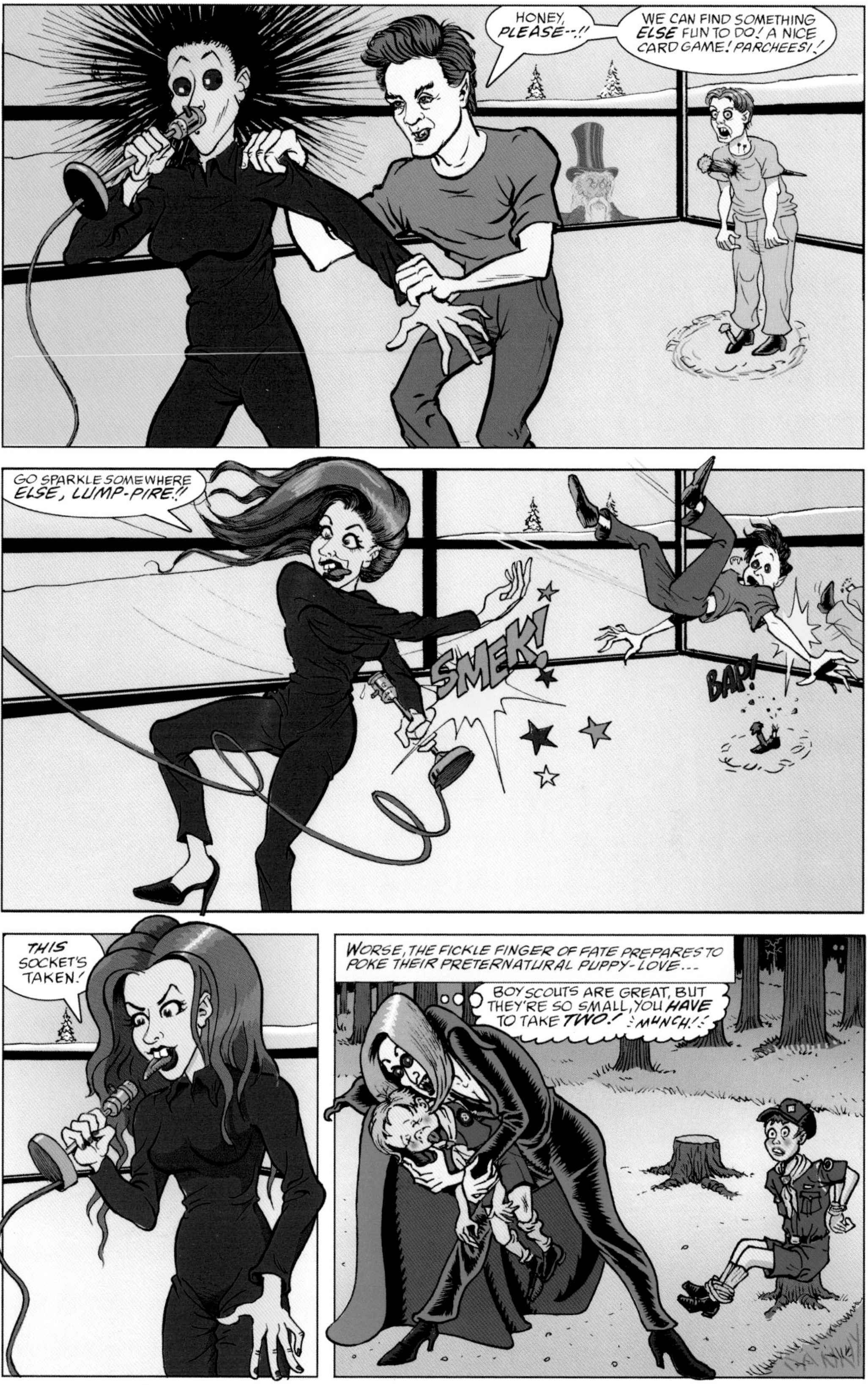

HONEY, PLEASE--!!
WE CAN FIND SOMETHING ELSE FUN TO DO! A NICE CARD GAME! PARCHEES!!
GO SPARKLE SOMEWHERE ELSE, LUMP-PIRE!!
SMEK!
BAP!
THIS SOCKET'S TAKEN!
WORSE, THE FICKLE FINGER OF FATE PREPARES TO POKE THEIR PRETERNATURAL PUPPY-LOVE...
BOY SCOUTS ARE GREAT, BUT THEY'RE SO SMALL, YOU HAVE TO TAKE TWO! MUNCH!

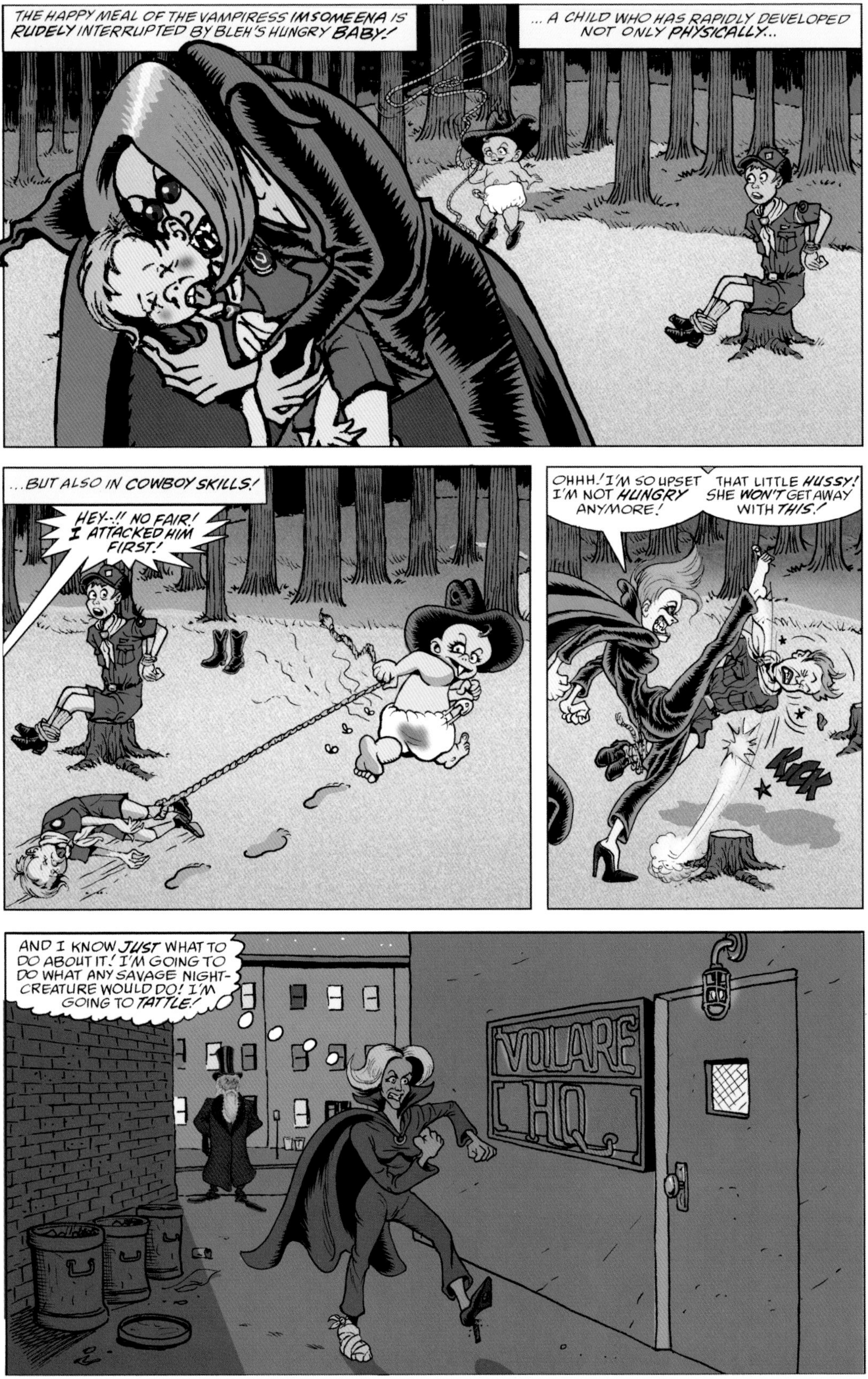
THE HAPPY MEAL OF THE VAMPIRESS IMSOMEENA IS RUDELY INTERRUPTED BY BLEH'S HUNGRY BABY!
...A CHILD WHO HAS RAPIDLY DEVELOPED NOT ONLY PHYSICALLY...
...BUT ALSO IN COWBOY SKILLS!
HEY--!! NO FAIR! I ATTACKED HIM FIRST!
OHHH! I'M SO UPSET I'M NOT HUNGRY ANYMORE!
THAT LITTLE HUSSY! SHE WON'T GET AWAY WITH THIS!
KICK
AND I KNOW JUST WHAT TO DO ABOUT IT! I'M GOING TO DO WHAT ANY SAVAGE NIGHT-CREATURE WOULD DO! I'M GOING TO TATTLE!
VOLARE HQ

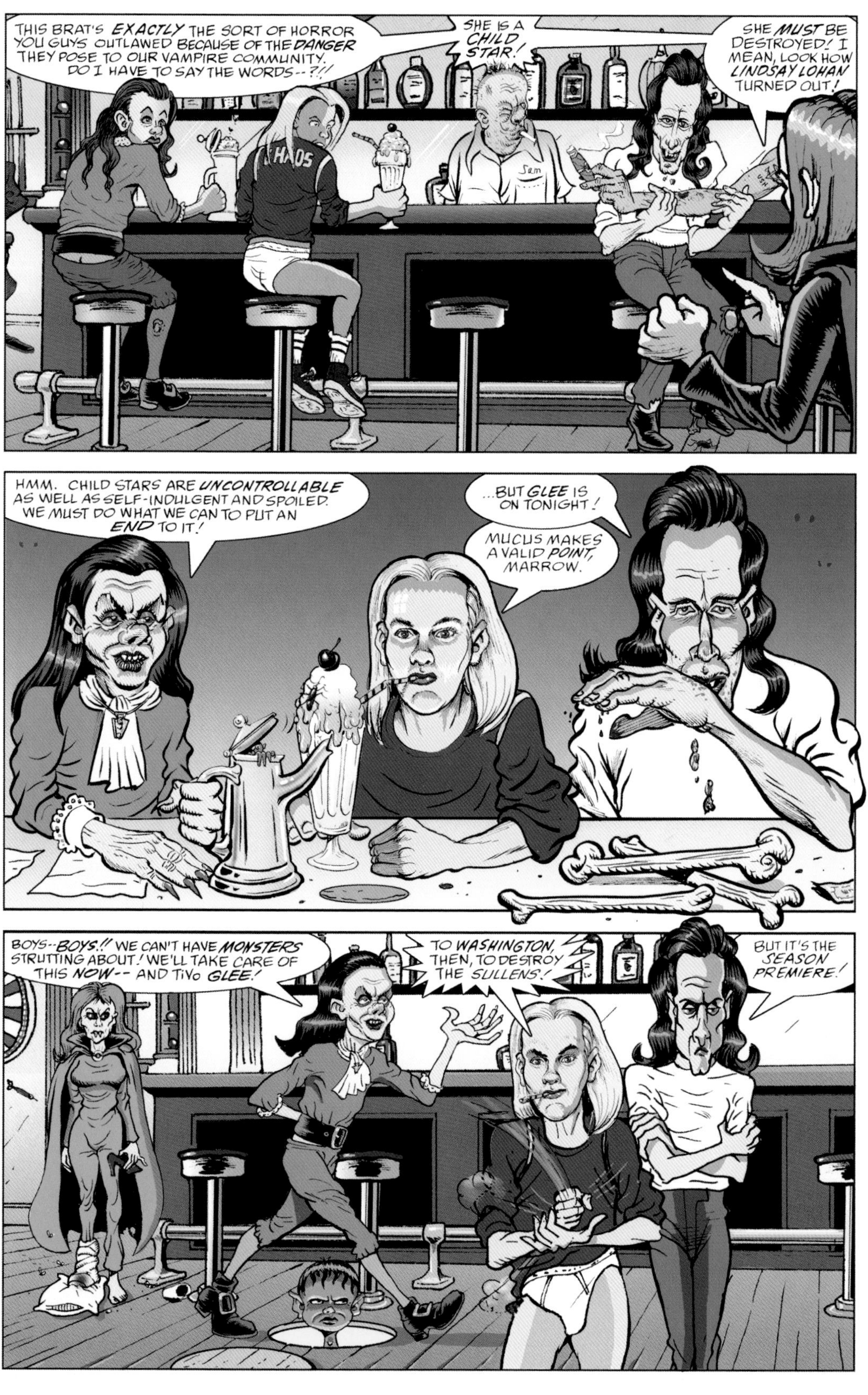
THIS BRAT'S EXACTLY THE SORT OF HORROR YOU GUYS OUTLAWED BECAUSE OF THE DANGER THEY POSE TO OUR VAMPIRE COMMUNITY. DO I HAVE TO SAY THE WORDS--?!!
SHE IS A CHILD STAR!
SHE MUST BE DESTROYED! I MEAN, LOOK HOW LINDSAY LOHAN TURNED OUT!
HMM. CHILD STARS ARE UNCONTROLLABLE AS WELL AS SELF-INDULGENT AND SPOILED. WE MUST DO WHAT WE CAN TO PUT AN END TO IT!
...BUT GLEE IS ON TONIGHT!
MUCUS MAKES A VALID POINT, MARROW.
BOYS--BOYS!! WE CAN'T HAVE MONSTERS STRUTTING ABOUT! WE'LL TAKE CARE OF THIS NOW-- AND TiVo GLEE!
TO WASHINGTON, THEN, TO DESTROY THE SULLENS!
BUT IT'S THE SEASON PREMIERE!

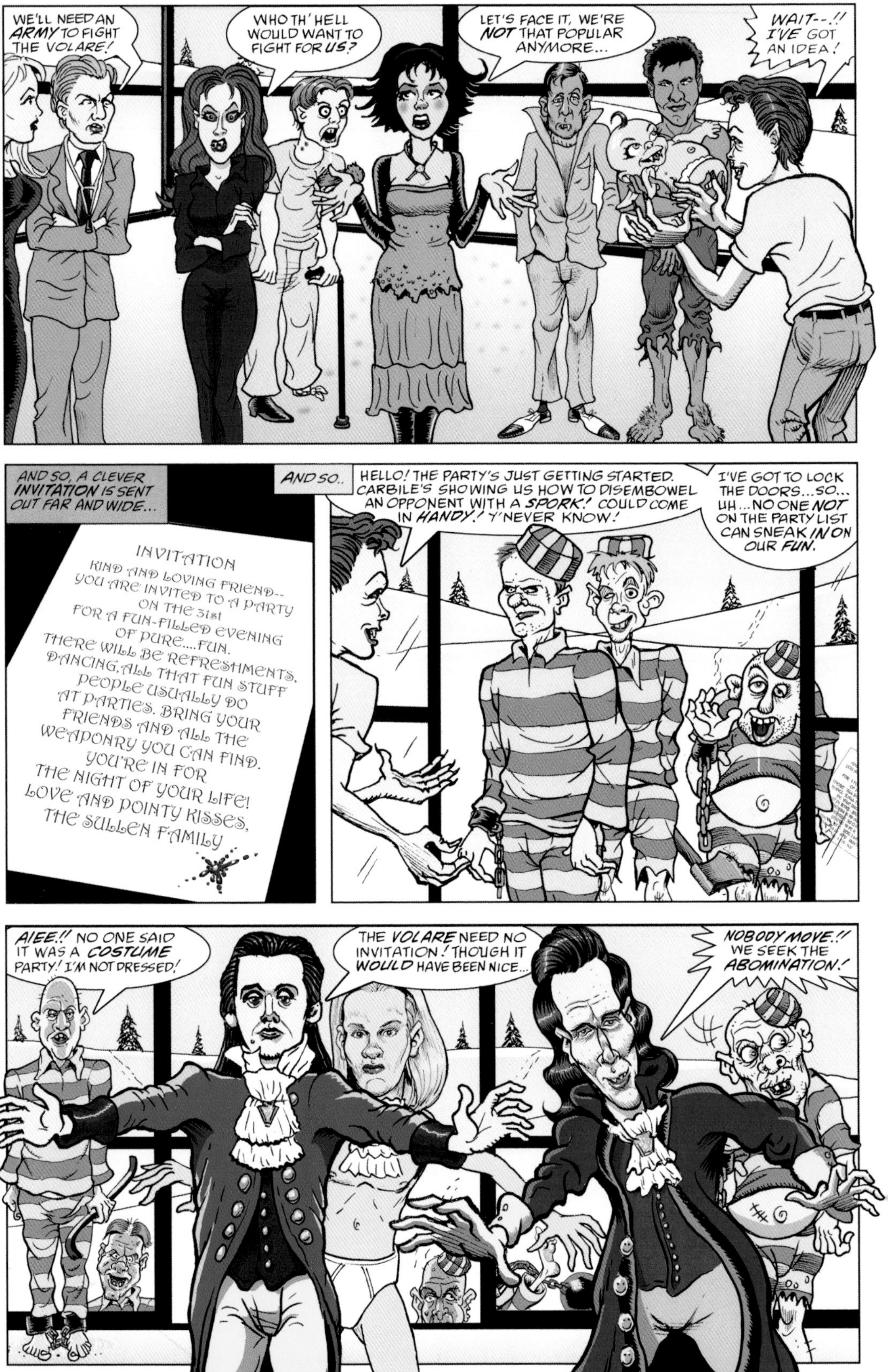
WE'LL NEED AN ARMY TO FIGHT THE VOLARE!
WHO TH' HELL WOULD WANT TO FIGHT FOR US?
LET'S FACE IT, WE'RE NOT THAT POPULAR ANYMORE...
WAIT--.!! I'VE GOT AN IDEA!
AND SO, A CLEVER INVITATION IS SENT OUT FAR AND WIDE...
INVITATION
KIND AND LOVING FRIEND--
YOU ARE INVITED TO A PARTY
ON THE 31st
FOR A FUN-FILLED EVENING
OF PURE....FUN.
THERE WILL BE REFRESHMENTS,
DANCING, ALL THAT FUN STUFF
PEOPLE USUALLY DO
AT PARTIES. BRING YOUR
FRIENDS AND ALL THE
WEAPONRY YOU CAN FIND.
YOU'RE IN FOR
THE NIGHT OF YOUR LIFE!
LOVE AND POINTY KISSES,
THE SULLEN FAMILY
AND SO..
HELLO! THE PARTY'S JUST GETTING STARTED. CARBILE'S SHOWING US HOW TO DISEMBOWEL AN OPPONENT WITH A SPORK! COULD COME IN HANDY! Y'NEVER KNOW!
I'VE GOT TO LOCK THE DOORS...SO... UH...NO ONE NOT ON THE PARTY LIST CAN SNEAK IN ON OUR FUN.
AIEE!! NO ONE SAID IT WAS A COSTUME PARTY! I'M NOT DRESSED!
THE VOLARE NEED NO INVITATION! THOUGH IT WOULD HAVE BEEN NICE...
NOBODY MOVE!! WE SEEK THE ABOMINATION!

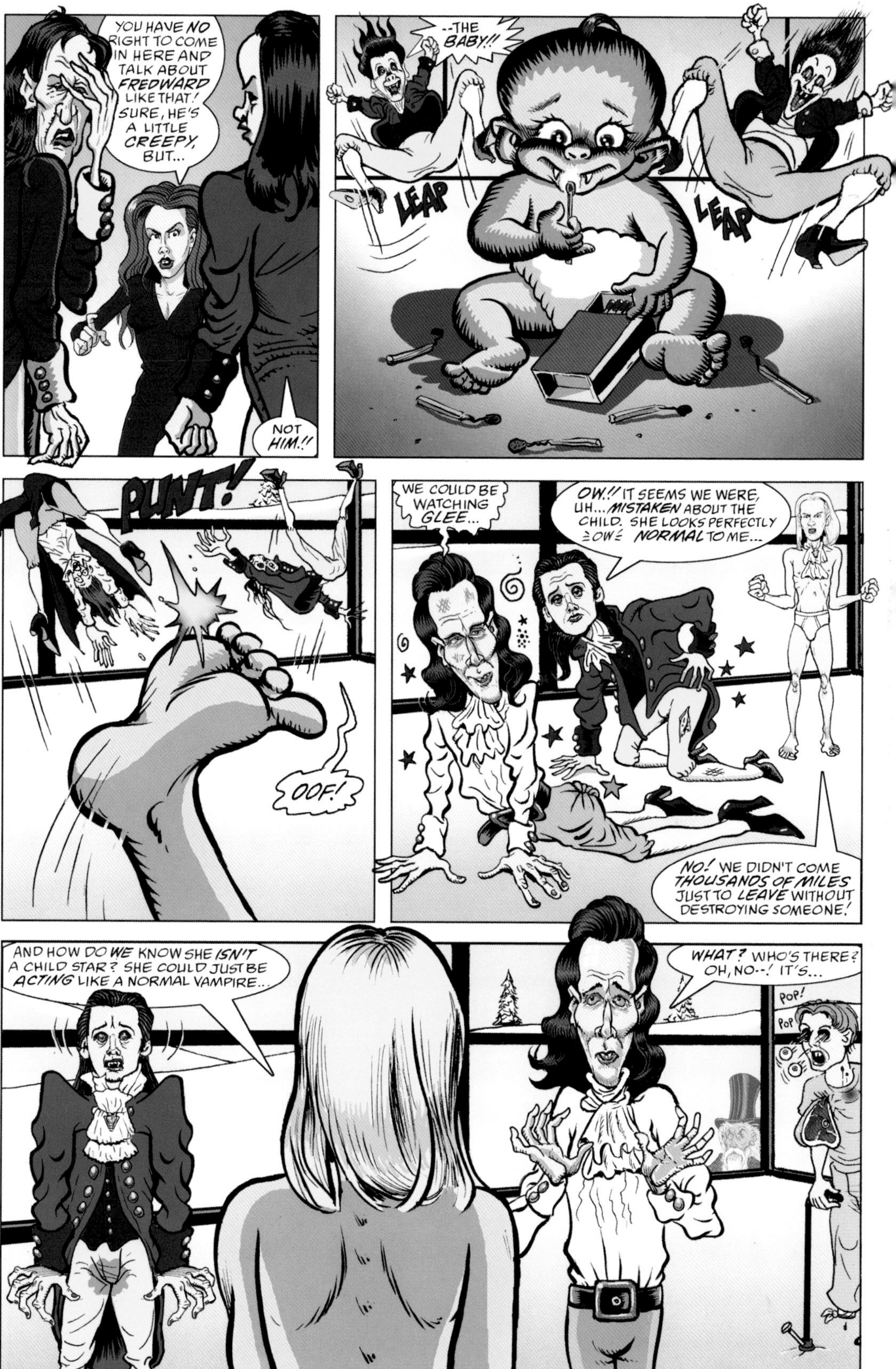
YOU HAVE NO RIGHT TO COME IN HERE AND TALK ABOUT FREDWARD LIKE THAT! SURE, HE'S A LITTLE CREEPY, BUT...
NOT HIM!!
--THE BABY!!
LEAP
LEAP
PUNT!
OOF!
WE COULD BE WATCHING GLEE...
OW!! IT SEEMS WE WERE, UH...MISTAKEN ABOUT THE CHILD. SHE LOOKS PERFECTLY ≥OW≤ NORMAL TO ME...
NO! WE DIDN'T COME THOUSANDS OF MILES JUST TO LEAVE WITHOUT DESTROYING SOMEONE!
AND HOW DO WE KNOW SHE ISN'T A CHILD STAR? SHE COULD JUST BE ACTING LIKE A NORMAL VAMPIRE...
WHAT? WHO'S THERE? OH, NO--! IT'S...
POP!
POP

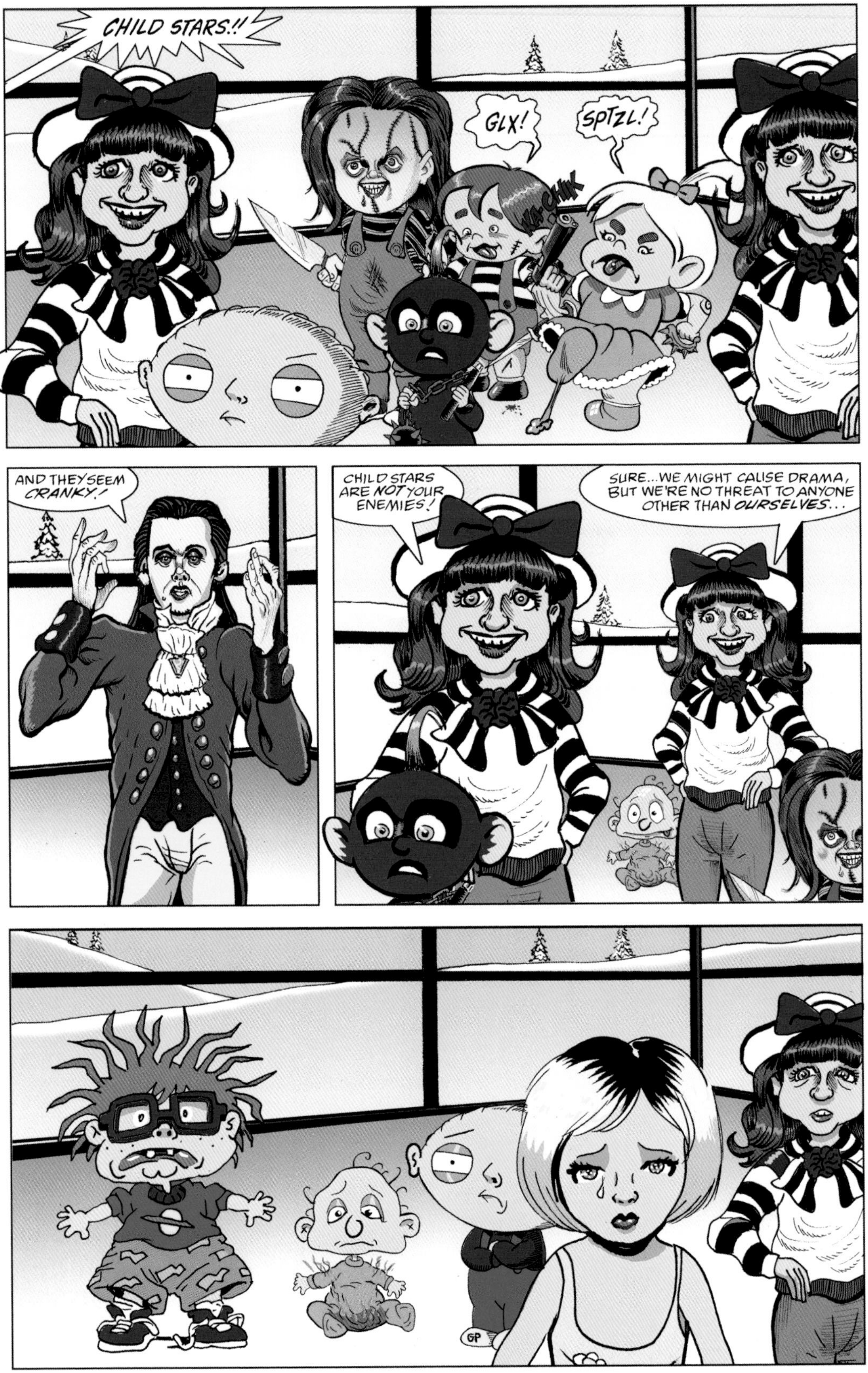
CHILD STARS!!
GLX!
SPTZL!
KA-CHIK
AND THEY SEEM *CRANKY!*
CHILD STARS ARE ***NOT*** YOUR ENEMIES!
SURE... WE MIGHT CAUSE DRAMA, BUT WE'RE NO THREAT TO ANYONE OTHER THAN ***OURSELVES***...
GP

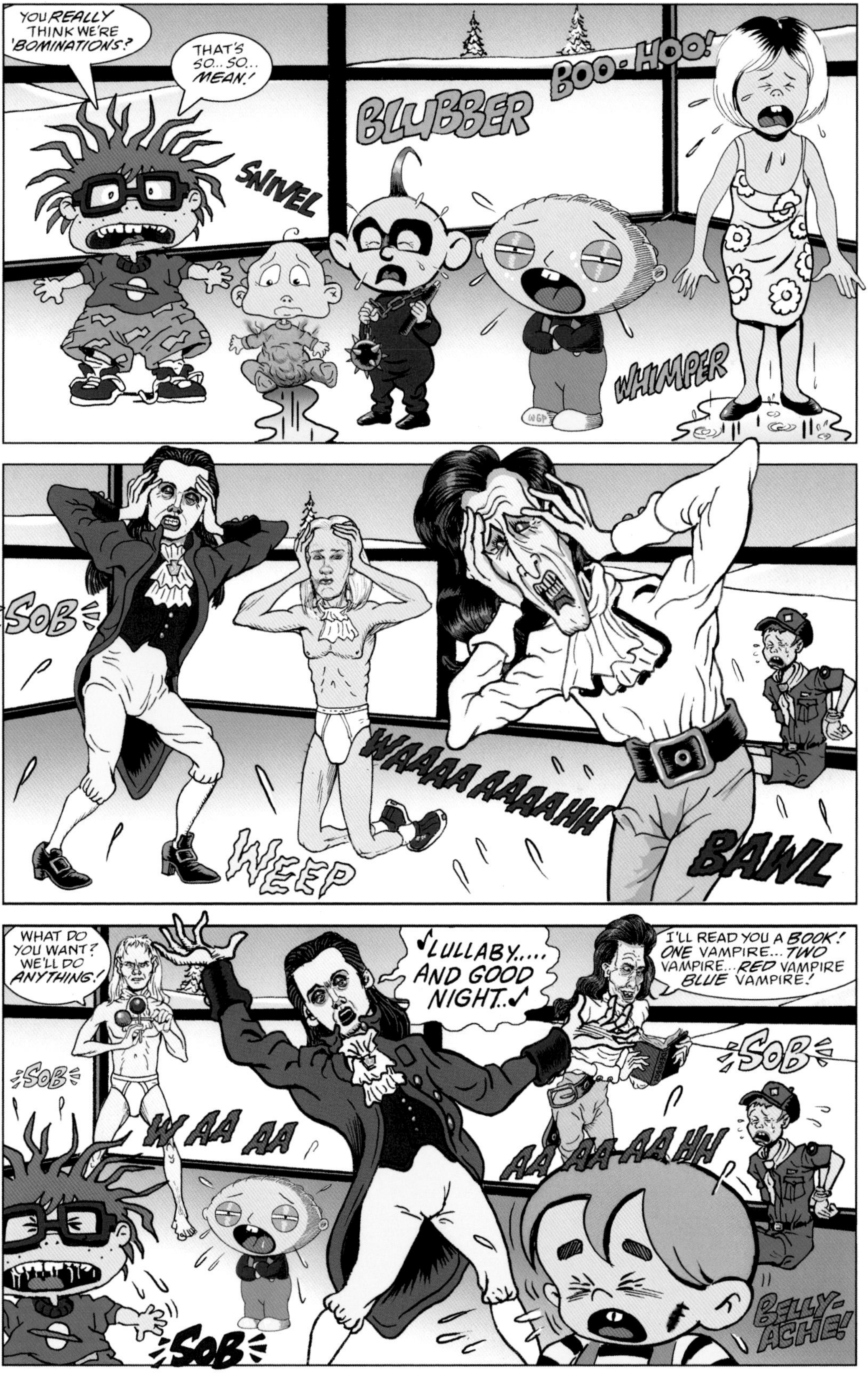
YOU REALLY THINK WE'RE 'BOMINATIONS?
THAT'S SO... SO... MEAN!
SNIVEL
BLUBBER
BOO-HOO!
WHIMPER
SOB
WAAAAAAAAAHH
WEEP
BAWL
WHAT DO YOU WANT? WE'LL DO ANYTHING!
♪LULLABY..... AND GOOD NIGHT..♪
I'LL READ YOU A BOOK! ONE VAMPIRE... TWO VAMPIRE... RED VAMPIRE BLUE VAMPIRE!
SOB
SOB
WAA AA AA AA AA AAHH
SOB
BELLY-ACHE!

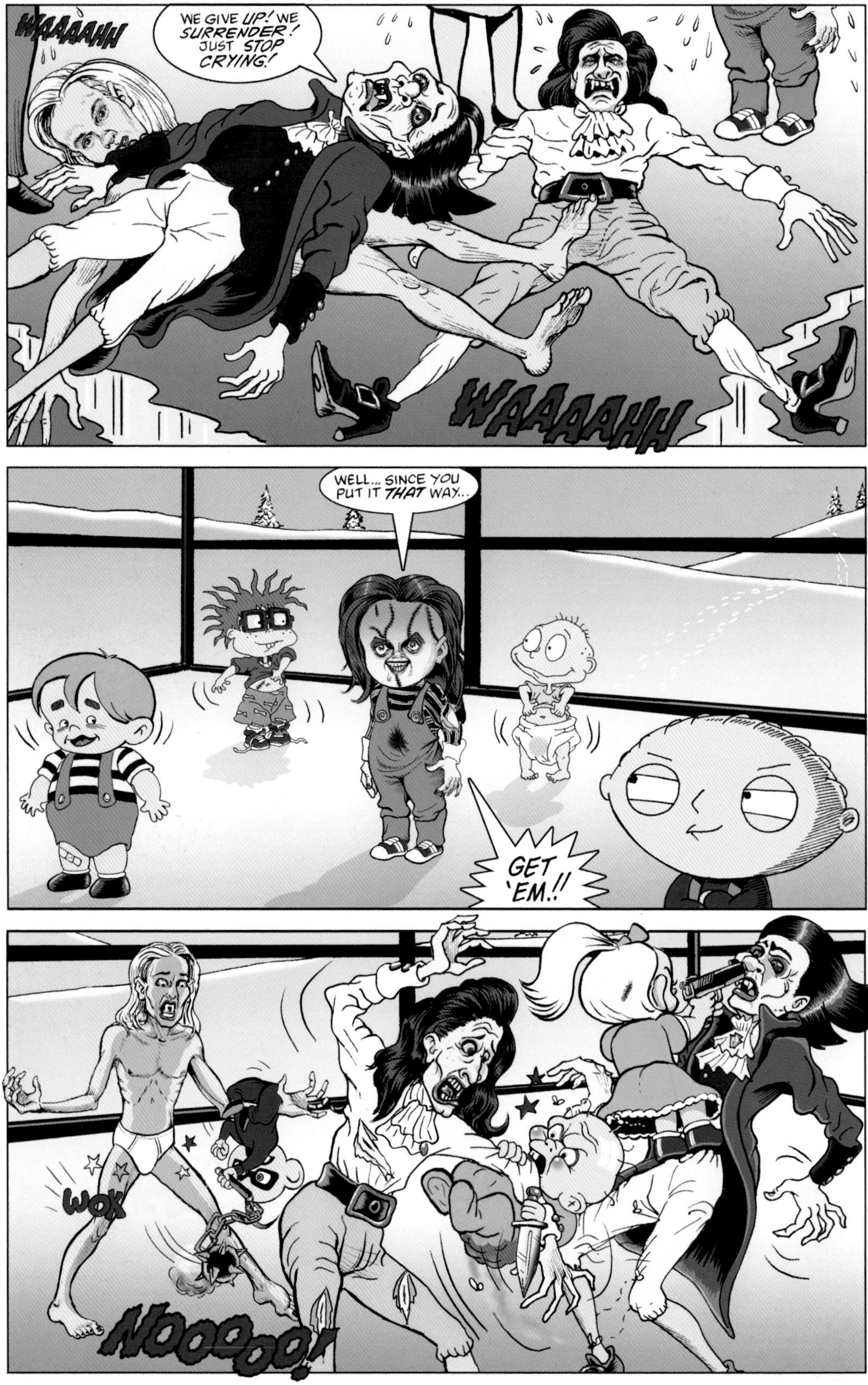
WAAAAHH
WE GIVE UP! WE SURRENDER! JUST STOP CRYING!
WAAAAHH
WELL... SINCE YOU PUT IT THAT WAY...
GET 'EM.!!
WOK
NOOOOO!

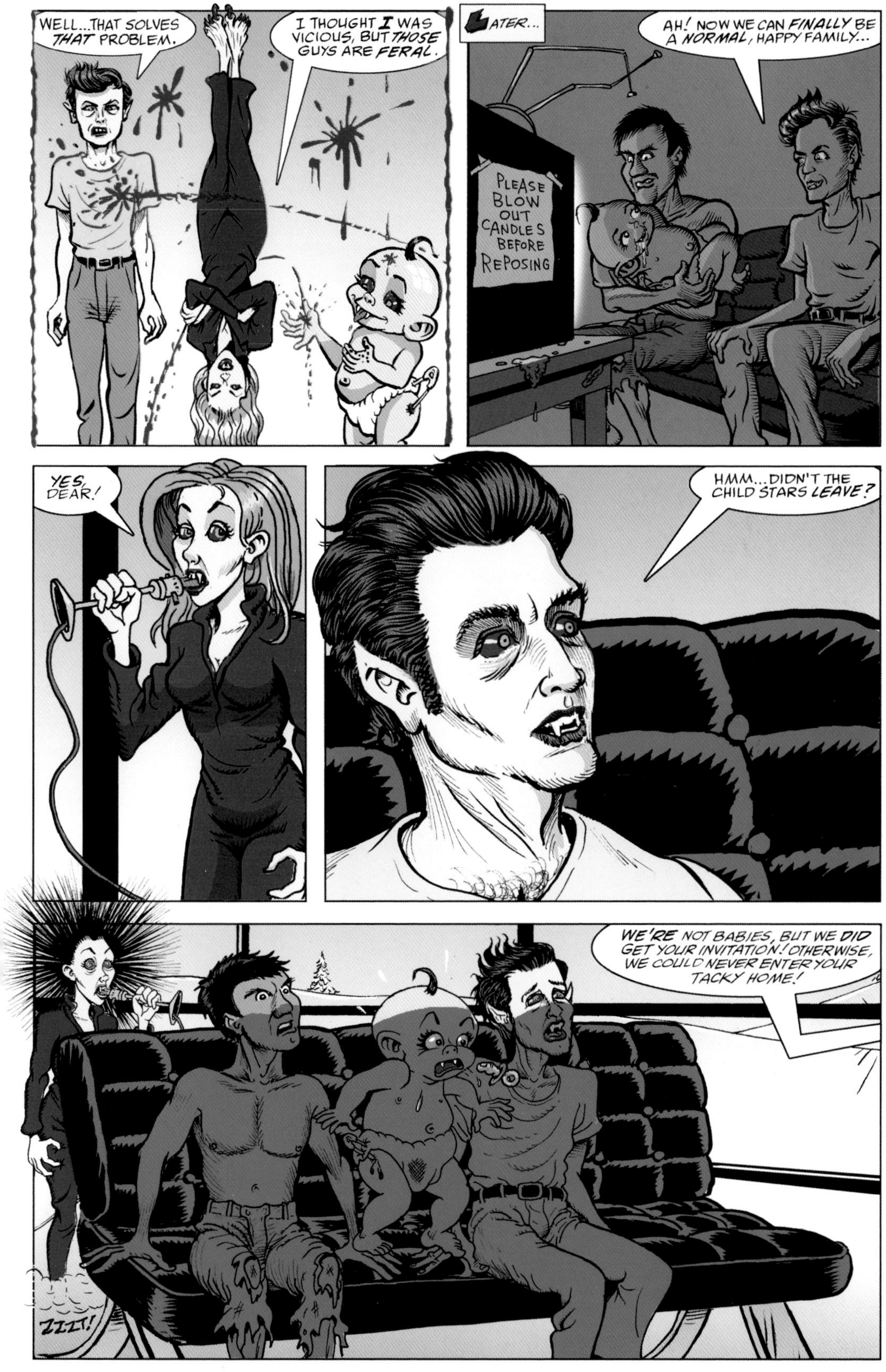
WELL...THAT SOLVES THAT PROBLEM.
I THOUGHT I WAS VICIOUS, BUT THOSE GUYS ARE FERAL.
LATER...
AH! NOW WE CAN FINALLY BE A NORMAL, HAPPY FAMILY...
PLEASE BLOW OUT CANDLES BEFORE REPOSING
YES, DEAR!
HMM...DIDN'T THE CHILD STARS LEAVE?
WE'RE NOT BABIES, BUT WE DID GET YOUR INVITATION! OTHERWISE, WE COULD NEVER ENTER YOUR TACKY HOME!
ZZZT!

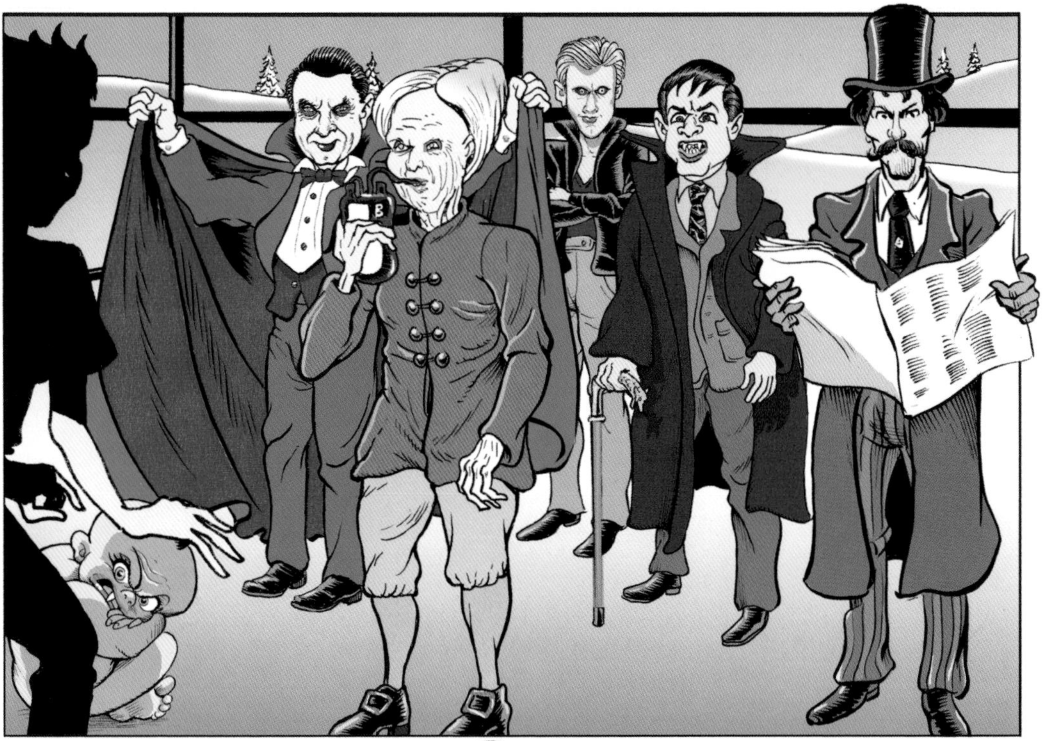

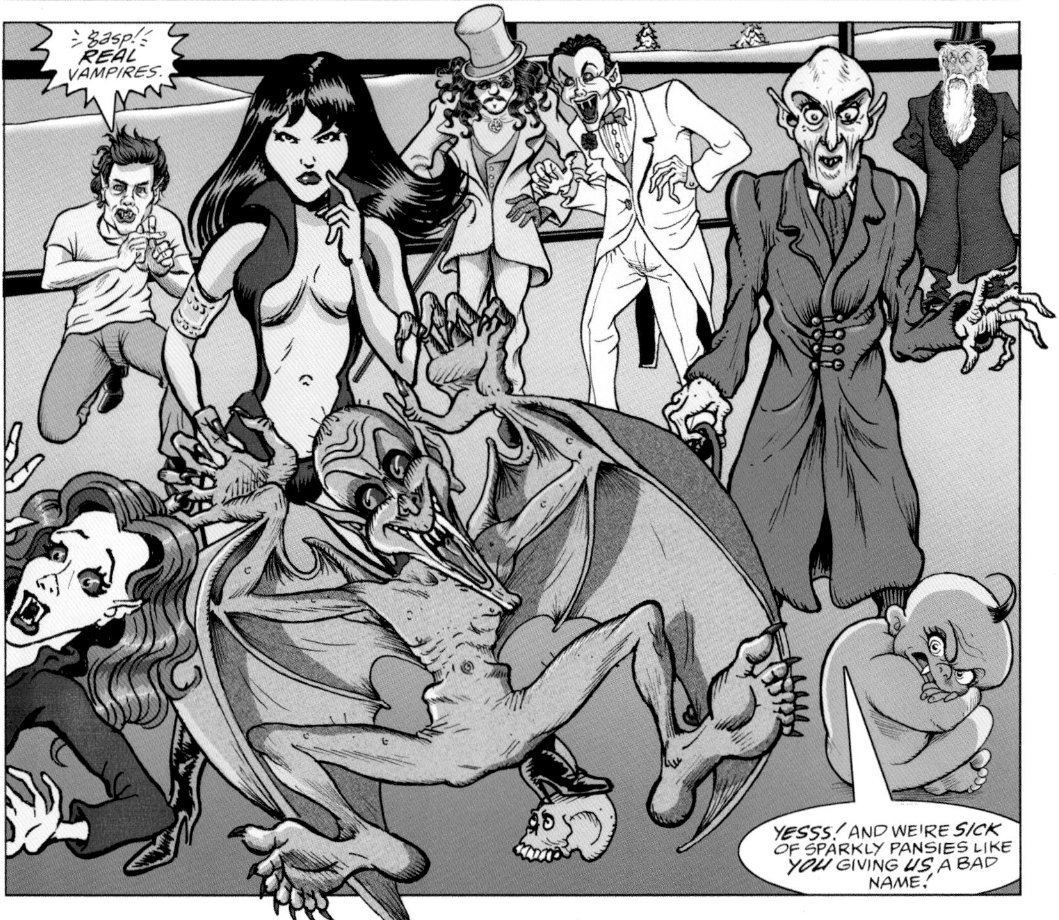
gasp! REAL VAMPIRES.
YESSS! AND WE'RE SICK OF SPARKLY PANSIES LIKE YOU GIVING US A BAD NAME!

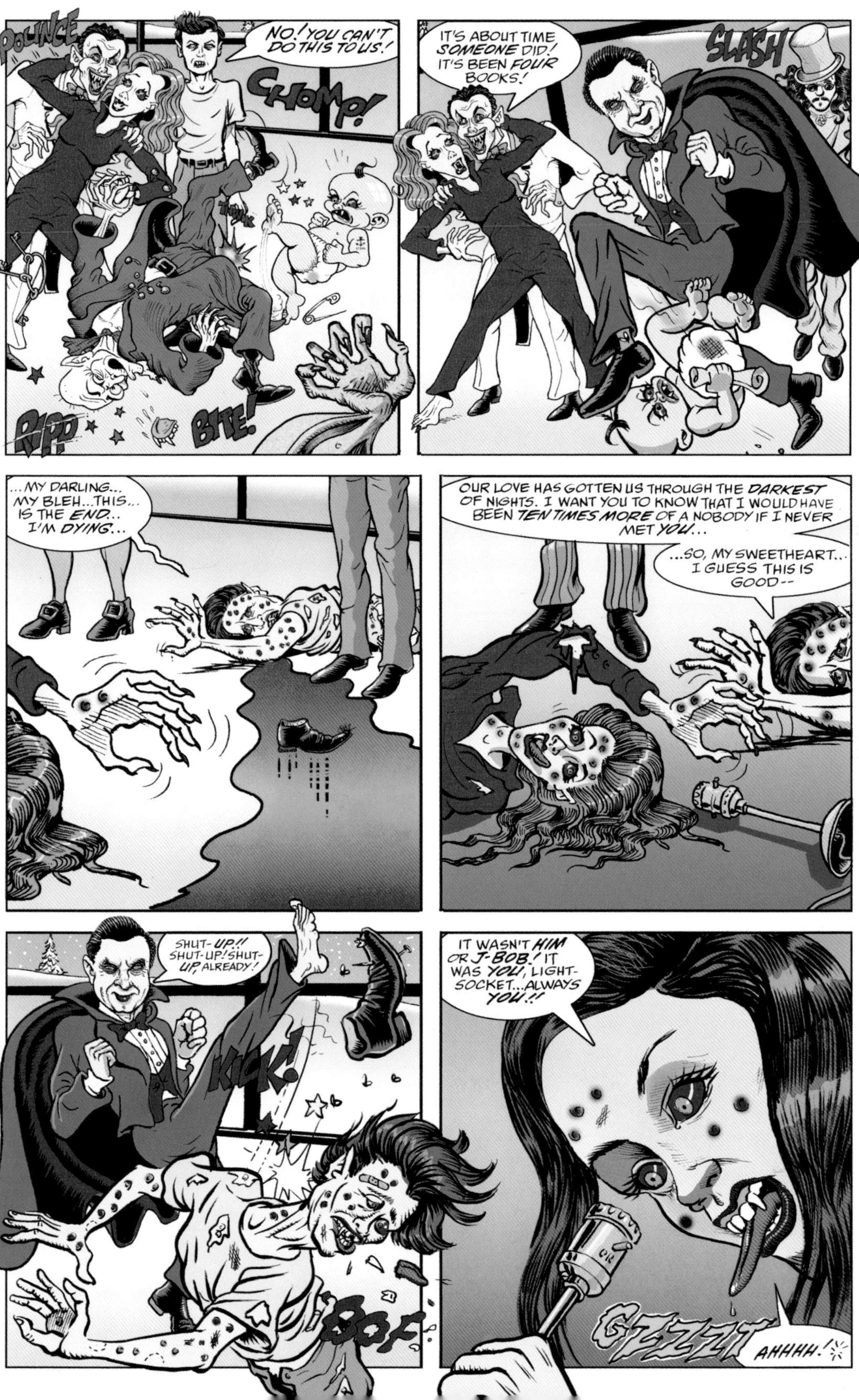
POUNCE
NO! YOU CAN'T DO THIS TO US!
CHOMP!
RIPP
BITE!
IT'S ABOUT TIME SOMEONE DID! IT'S BEEN FOUR BOOKS!
SLASH
...MY DARLING... MY BLEH...THIS... IS THE END... I'M DYING...
OUR LOVE HAS GOTTEN US THROUGH THE DARKEST OF NIGHTS. I WANT YOU TO KNOW THAT I WOULD HAVE BEEN TEN TIMES MORE OF A NOBODY IF I NEVER MET YOU...
...SO, MY SWEETHEART... I GUESS THIS IS GOOD--
SHUT-UP!! SHUT-UP! SHUT-UP, ALREADY!
KICK!
OOF
IT WASN'T HIM OR J-BOB! IT WAS YOU!, LIGHT-SOCKET...ALWAYS YOU!!
GZZZT
AHHHH!

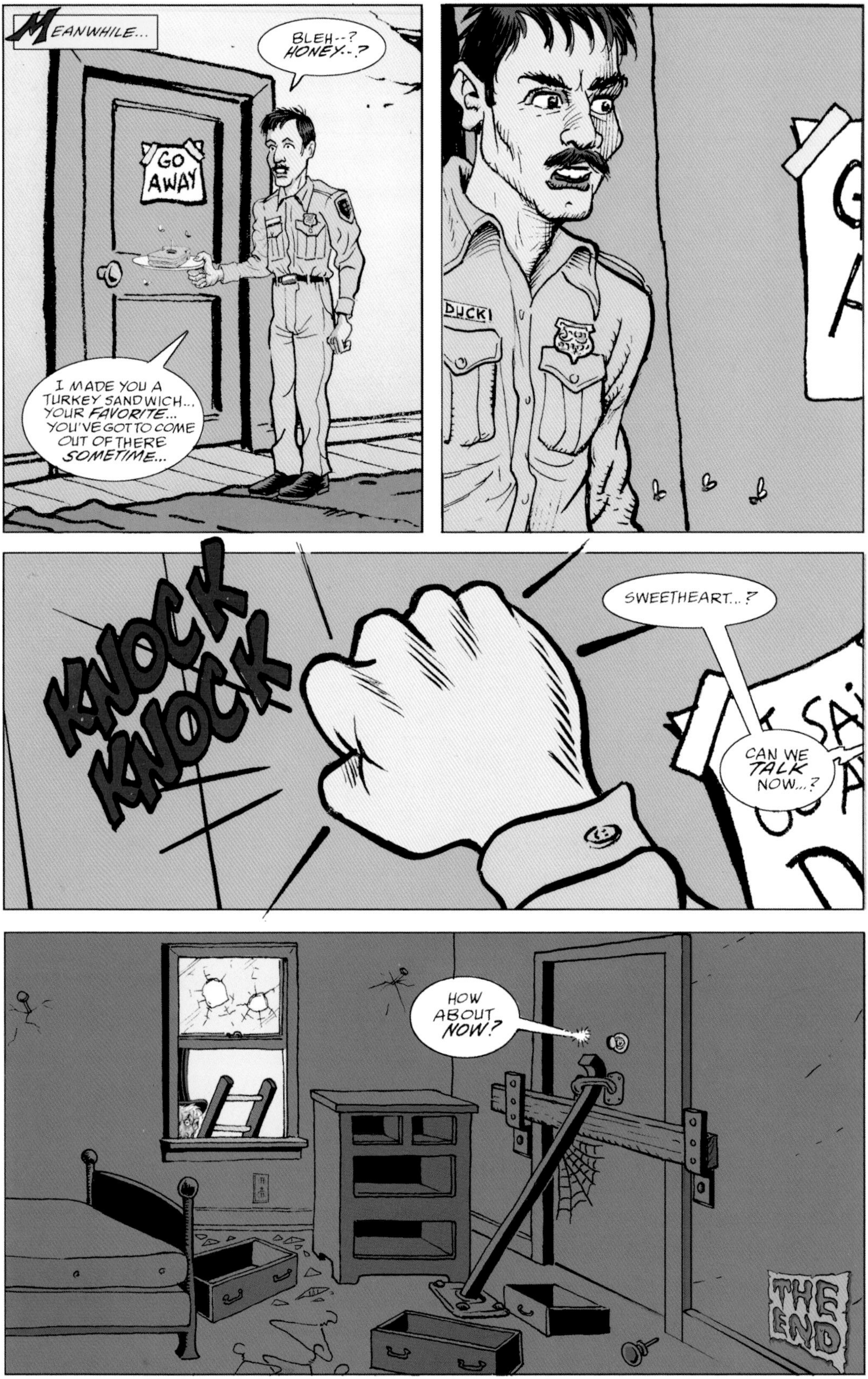
MEANWHILE...
BLEH--? HONEY--?
I MADE YOU A TURKEY SANDWICH... YOUR FAVORITE... YOU'VE GOT TO COME OUT OF THERE SOMETIME...
GO AWAY
DUCKI
KNOCK KNOCK
SWEETHEART...?
CAN WE TALK NOW...?
HOW ABOUT NOW?
THE END

WATCH OUT FOR PAPERCUTZ

Welcome to supernaturally seductive and silly second volume of PAPERCUTZ SLICES, the new graphic novel series dedicated to poking fun at your favorite pop culture phenomenona. I'm Jim Salicrup, your glow-in-dark Editor-in-Chief, here to provide a little behind-the-scenes info on both Papercutz and PAPERCUTZ SLICES, and to generally fill up another page.

For those of you wondering what Papercutz is, let me quickly explain it's not the nasty little nicks you get from sharp sheets of paper. Rather Papercutz is dedicated to publishing great graphic novels for all ages—it says so right in that little box on all our back covers. At the recent Miami Book Fair International your humble (acting) Editor-in-Chief manned the Papercutz booth, and got all sorts of fascinating feedback on our books. For example, the covers of TALES FROM THE CRYPT #8 "Diary of a Stinky Dead Kid" and PAPERCUTZ SLICES #1 "Harry Potty and the Deathly Boring" attracted a lot of favorable attention. Kids of all ages would point at the covers and laugh. And they were laughing with them, and not at them. People seemed to not only get that we were creating comics that poked fun at popular books and movies, but they really liked it.

There were a few kids at the Miami Book Fair International who didn't quite get it, though. They thought we were being very, very mean and were making fun of their favorite characters. Well, yes, we were making fun of them, but we weren't trying to be mean. We were just trying to be funny. The people who will probably enjoy our parodies most, are probably the ones who are knowledgeable enough about our targets to understand all of the jokes.

Surprisingly, once people at the Miami Book Fair International got that we published a couple of parody graphic novels, a few of them assumed that ALL of the Papercutz graphic novels were parodies. I had to gently explain, that despite titles such as NANCY DREW The New Case Files #1 "Vampire Slayer," THE HARDY BOYS The New Case Files #1 "Crawling With Zombies," and THE SMURFS #1 "The Purple Smurfs," these graphic novels featured the real deals. The REAL Nancy Drew, the REAL Hardy Boys, and the REAL Smurfs. Honest.

The Miami Book Fair International attendees were great—we loved hearing their feedback. But you don't have to attend a book fair to tell us what YOU think. Just email your feedback to salicrup@papercutz.com or write me an actual letter, and mail it to: PAPERCUTZ SLICES, 40 Exchange Place, Suite 1308, New York, NY 10005. We really want to hear what you think of "breaking down" and what other books, tv shows, or movies you'd like to see Stefan Petrucha and Rick Parker parody next.

Speaking of parodies, we're including an exclusive excerpt from TALES FROM THE CRYPT #9 "Wickeder" on the next few pages. It's written by Maia Kinney-Petrucha and Stefan Petrucha, the same wicked writers that wrote "breaking down," drawn by Diego Jourdan, with an introduction featuring horror hosts the Crypt-Keeper and the Vault-Keeper, written by Ye Olde Editor, and drawn by Rick Parker, the artist who drew "breaking down." TALES FROM THE CRYPT #9 "Wickeder" is on sale now at bookstores, comicbook stores, and online booksellers. It also features the return of the Stinky Dead Kid, and a short terror-tale entitled "Kill, Baby, Kill."

Before we run out of room, we're bursting to tell you that Stefan Petrucha and Rick Parker have selected the target for their next gut-busting parody. Be sure to check your favorite bookseller in August 2011 for PAPERCUTZ SLICES #3 "Percy Jerkson and the Ovolactovegetarians".

May the Farce be with you,

JIM

The Stinky Dead Kid Returns In...

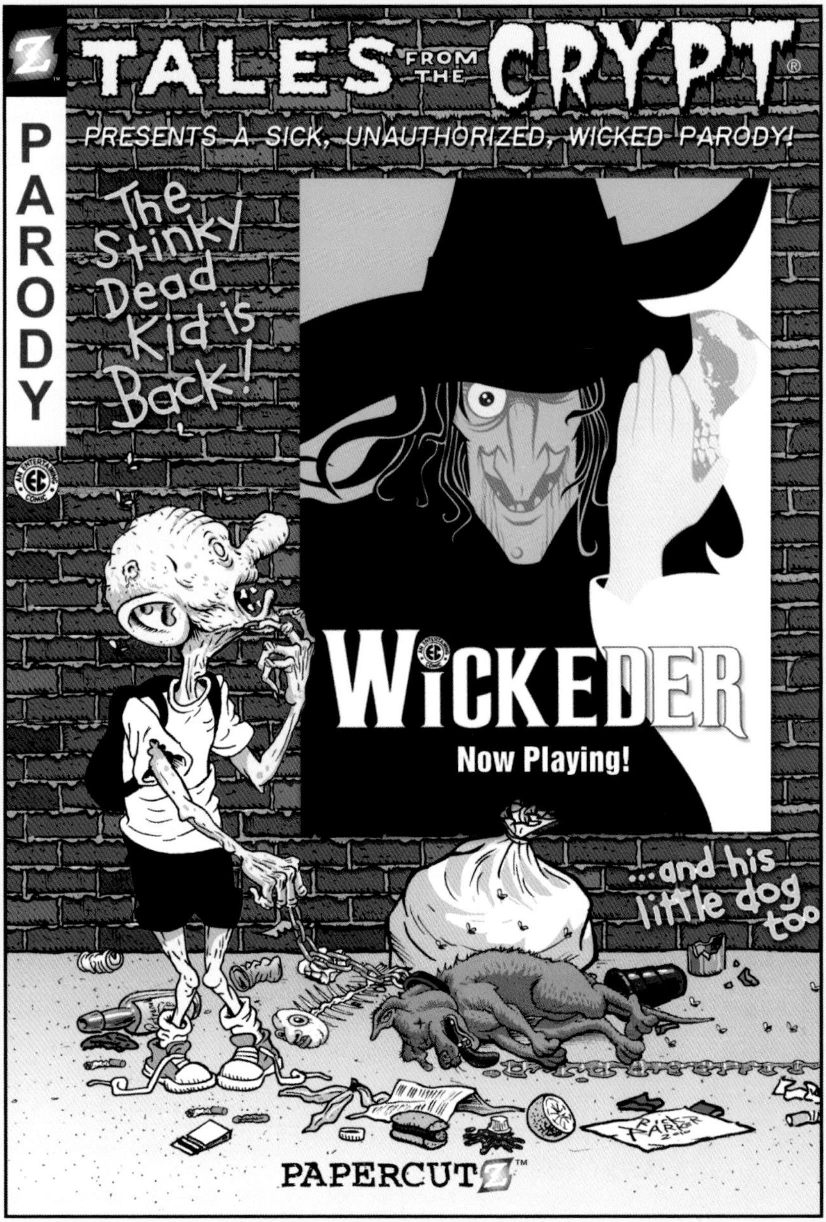
TALES FROM THE CRYPT®
PARODY
PRESENTS A SICK, UNAUTHORIZED, WICKED PARODY!
The Stinky Dead Kid is Back!
WICKEDER
Now Playing!
...and his little dog too
PAPERCUTZ™

On Sale Now!

SPECIAL PREVIEW OF
TALES FROM THE CRYPT #9 "WICKEDER"—

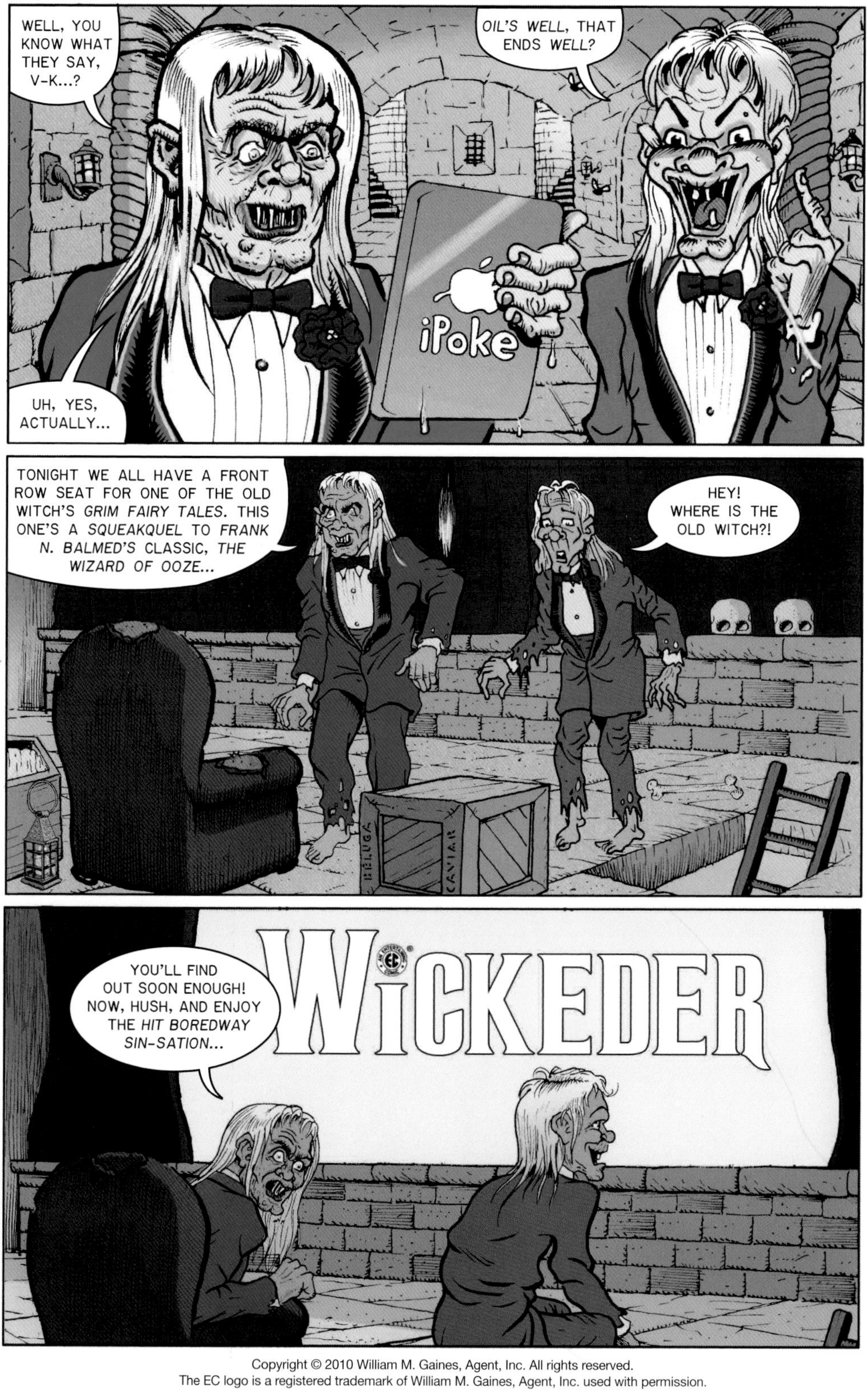
WELL, YOU KNOW WHAT THEY SAY, V-K...?
OIL'S WELL, THAT ENDS WELL?
UH, YES, ACTUALLY...
iPoke
TONIGHT WE ALL HAVE A FRONT ROW SEAT FOR ONE OF THE OLD WITCH'S GRIM FAIRY TALES. THIS ONE'S A SQUEAKQUEL TO FRANK N. BALMED'S CLASSIC, THE WIZARD OF OOZE...
HEY! WHERE IS THE OLD WITCH?!
BELUGA
CAVIAR
WICKEDER
YOU'LL FIND OUT SOON ENOUGH! NOW, HUSH, AND ENJOY THE HIT BOREDWAY SIN-SATION...

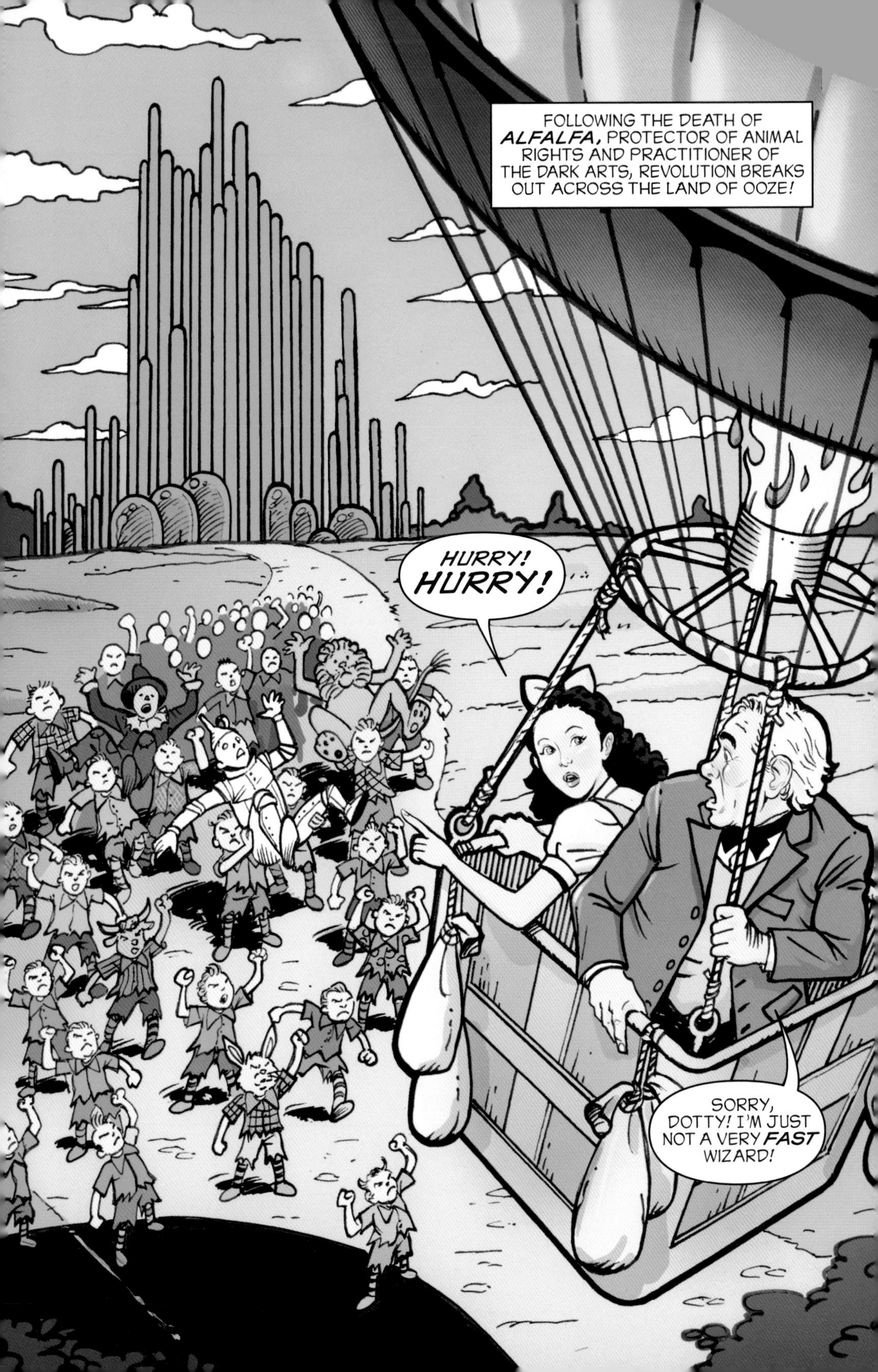
FOLLOWING THE DEATH OF ALFALFA, PROTECTOR OF ANIMAL RIGHTS AND PRACTITIONER OF THE DARK ARTS, REVOLUTION BREAKS OUT ACROSS THE LAND OF OOZE!
HURRY! HURRY!
SORRY, DOTTY! I'M JUST NOT A VERY FAST WIZARD!

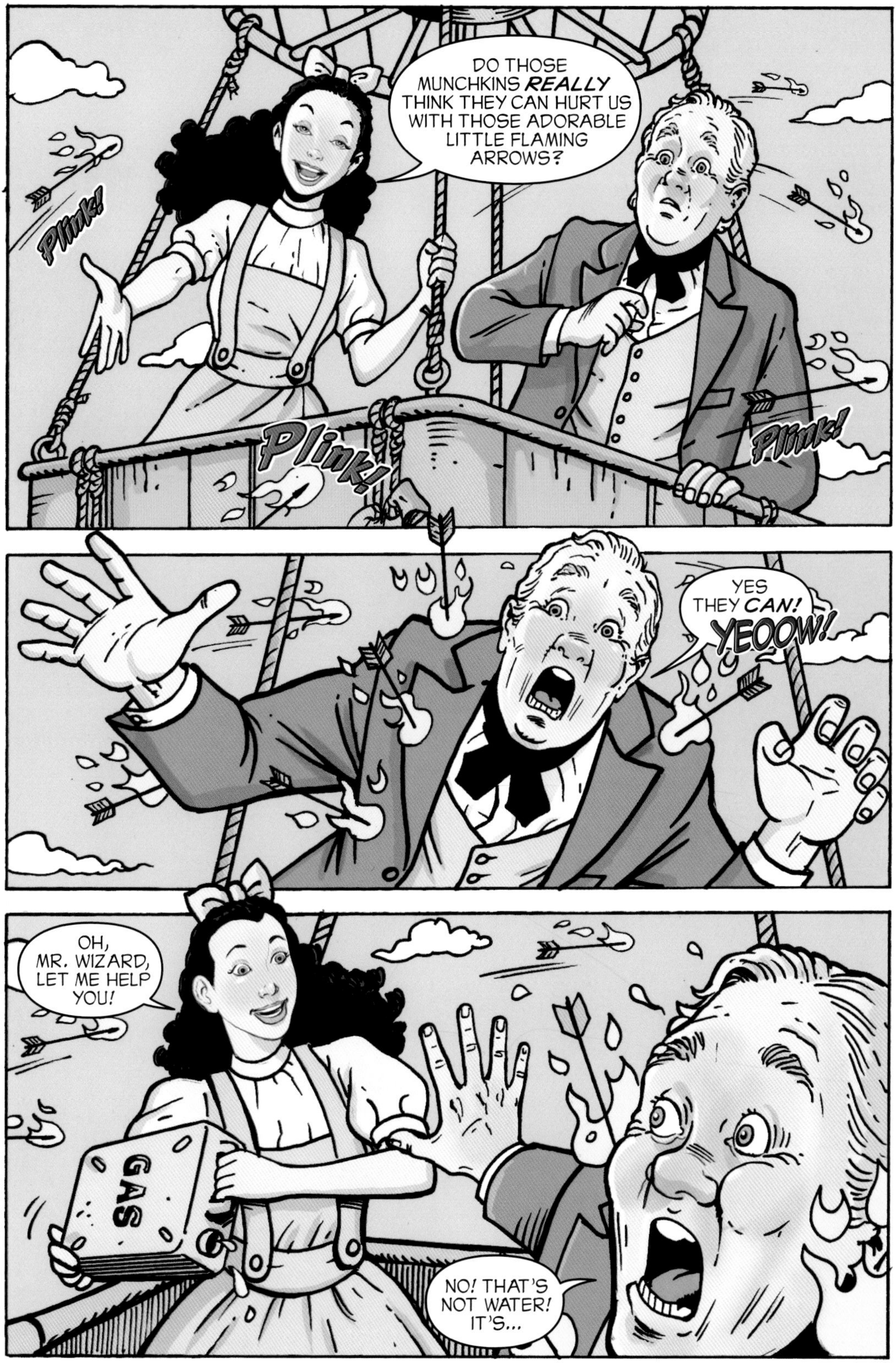
DO THOSE MUNCHKINS REALLY THINK THEY CAN HURT US WITH THOSE ADORABLE LITTLE FLAMING ARROWS?
Plink!
Plink!
Plink!
YES THEY CAN!
YEOOW!
OH, MR. WIZARD, LET ME HELP YOU!
GAS
NO! THAT'S NOT WATER! IT'S...

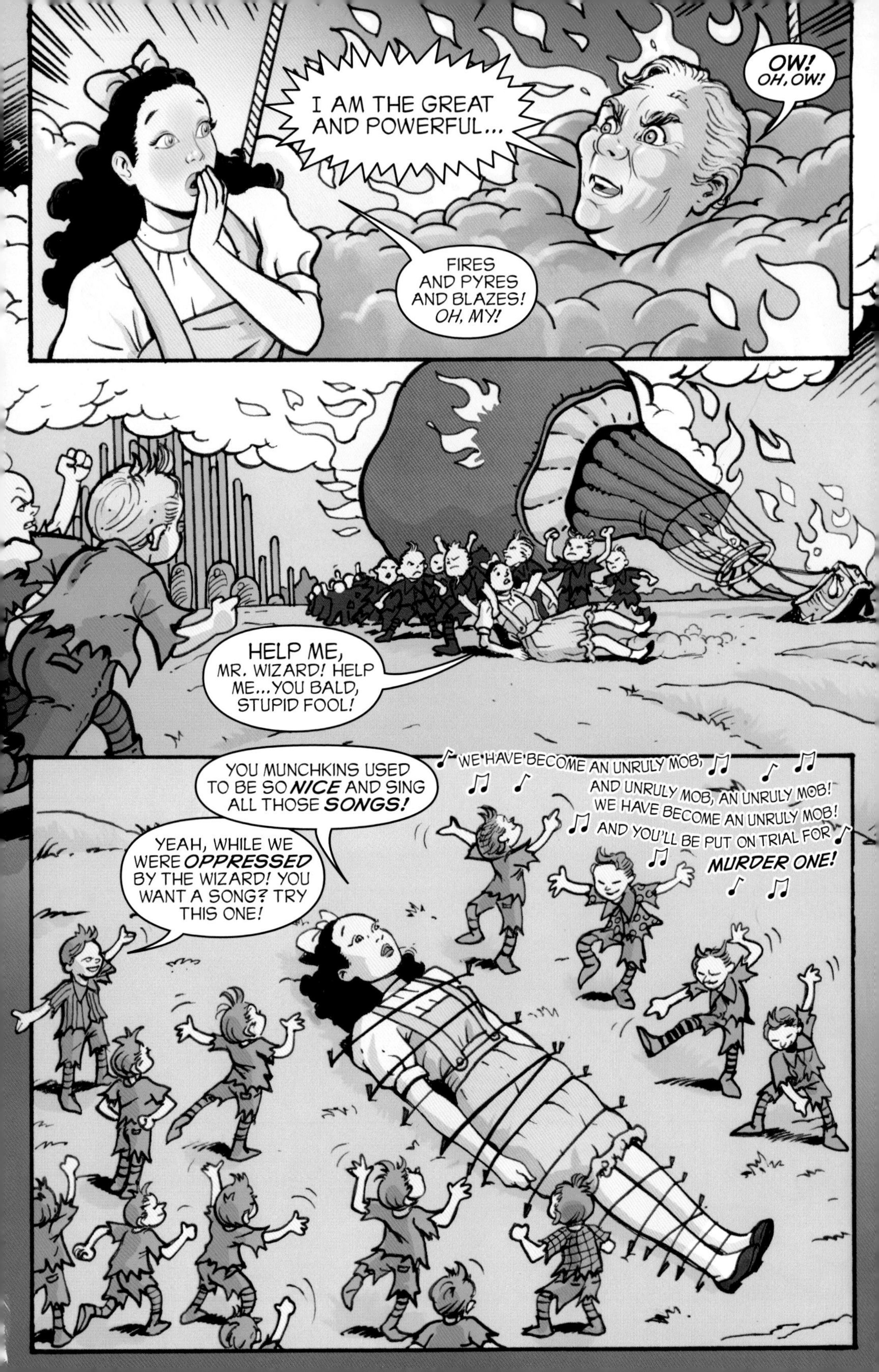
I AM THE GREAT AND POWERFUL...
OW! OH, OW!
FIRES AND PYRES AND BLAZES! OH, MY!
HELP ME, MR. WIZARD! HELP ME...YOU BALD, STUPID FOOL!
YOU MUNCHKINS USED TO BE SO NICE AND SING ALL THOSE SONGS!
YEAH, WHILE WE WERE OPPRESSED BY THE WIZARD! YOU WANT A SONG? TRY THIS ONE!
WE HAVE BECOME AN UNRULY MOB,
AND UNRULY MOB, AN UNRULY MOB!
WE HAVE BECOME AN UNRULY MOB!
AND YOU'LL BE PUT ON TRIAL FOR
MURDER ONE!

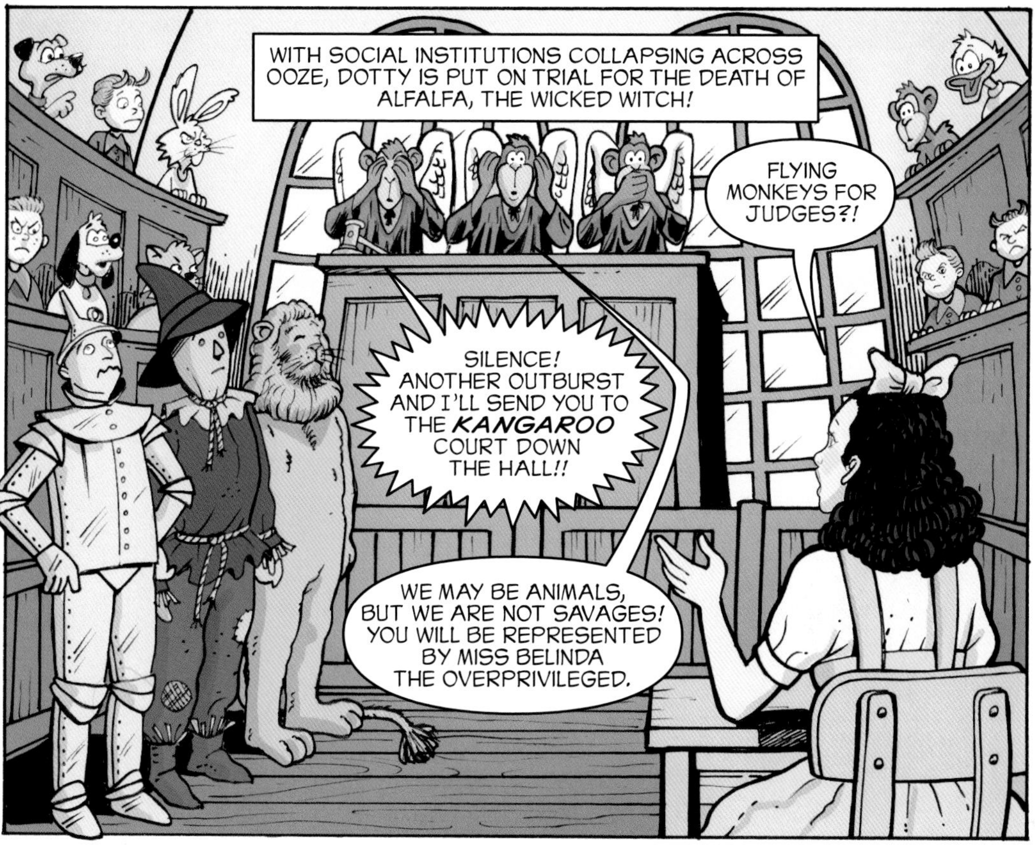
WITH SOCIAL INSTITUTIONS COLLAPSING ACROSS OOZE, DOTTY IS PUT ON TRIAL FOR THE DEATH OF ALFALFA, THE WICKED WITCH!
FLYING MONKEYS FOR JUDGES?!
SILENCE! ANOTHER OUTBURST AND I'LL SEND YOU TO THE *KANGAROO* COURT DOWN THE HALL!!
WE MAY BE ANIMALS, BUT WE ARE NOT SAVAGES! YOU WILL BE REPRESENTED BY MISS BELINDA THE OVERPRIVILEGED.

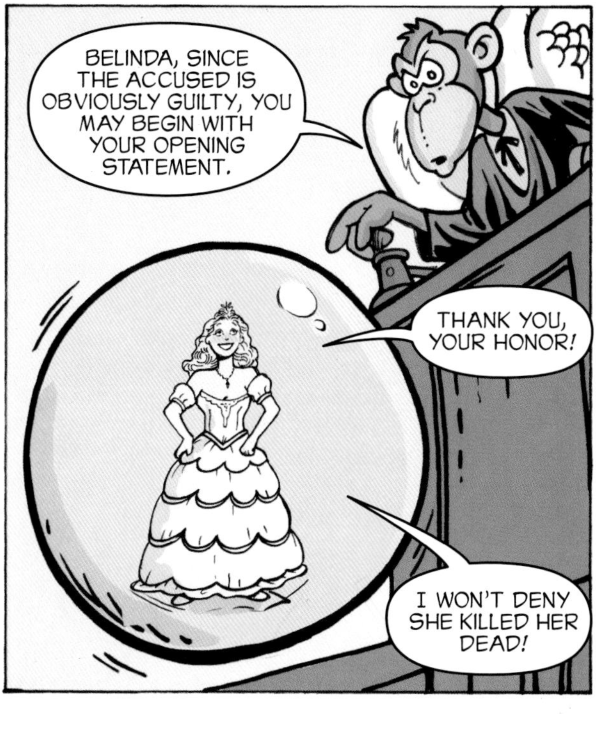
BELINDA, SINCE THE ACCUSED IS OBVIOUSLY GUILTY, YOU MAY BEGIN WITH YOUR OPENING STATEMENT.
THANK YOU, YOUR HONOR!
I WON'T DENY SHE KILLED HER DEAD!

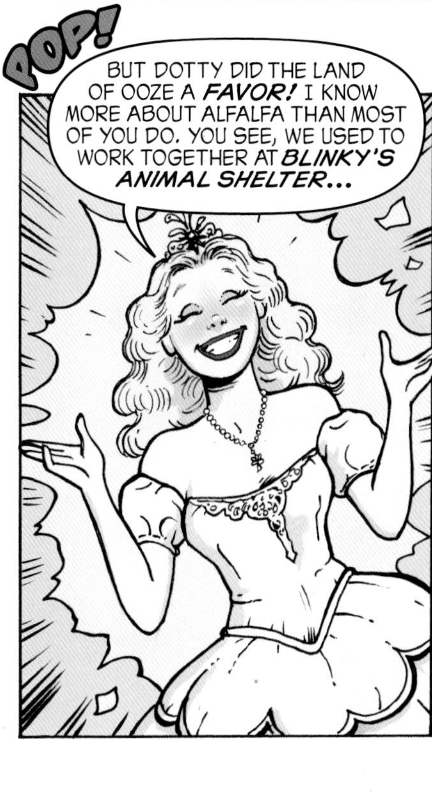
POP!
BUT DOTTY DID THE LAND OF OOZE A *FAVOR!* I KNOW MORE ABOUT ALFALFA THAN MOST OF YOU DO. YOU SEE, WE USED TO WORK TOGETHER AT *BLINKY'S ANIMAL SHELTER...*

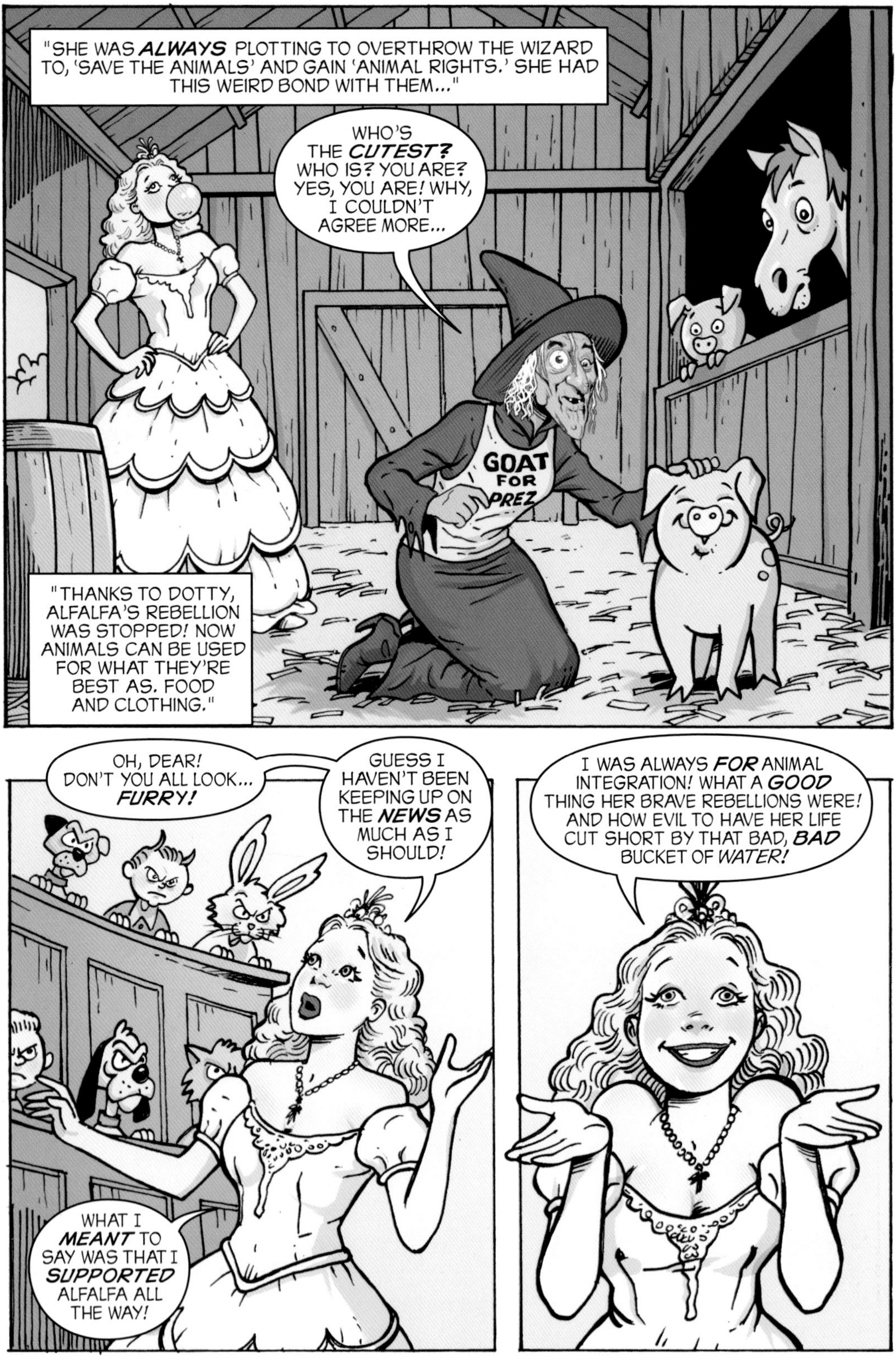
"SHE WAS ALWAYS PLOTTING TO OVERTHROW THE WIZARD TO, 'SAVE THE ANIMALS' AND GAIN 'ANIMAL RIGHTS.' SHE HAD THIS WEIRD BOND WITH THEM..."
WHO'S THE CUTEST? WHO IS? YOU ARE? YES, YOU ARE! WHY, I COULDN'T AGREE MORE...
GOAT FOR PREZ
"THANKS TO DOTTY, ALFALFA'S REBELLION WAS STOPPED! NOW ANIMALS CAN BE USED FOR WHAT THEY'RE BEST AS. FOOD AND CLOTHING."
OH, DEAR! DON'T YOU ALL LOOK... FURRY!
GUESS I HAVEN'T BEEN KEEPING UP ON THE NEWS AS MUCH AS I SHOULD!
WHAT I MEANT TO SAY WAS THAT I SUPPORTED ALFALFA ALL THE WAY!
I WAS ALWAYS FOR ANIMAL INTEGRATION! WHAT A GOOD THING HER BRAVE REBELLIONS WERE! AND HOW EVIL TO HAVE HER LIFE CUT SHORT BY THAT BAD, BAD BUCKET OF WATER!

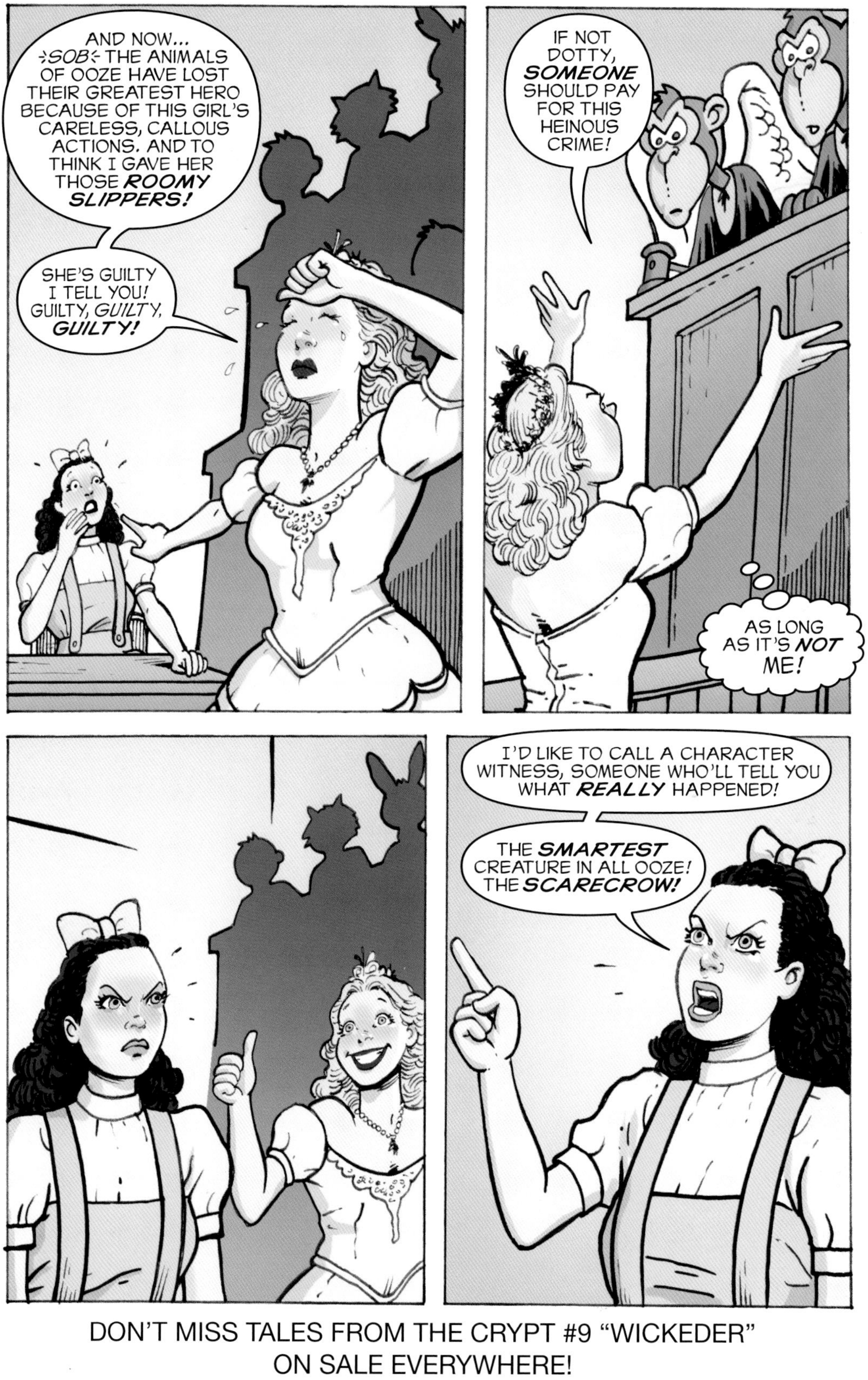
AND NOW... ⊰SOB⊱ THE ANIMALS OF OOZE HAVE LOST THEIR GREATEST HERO BECAUSE OF THIS GIRL'S CARELESS, CALLOUS ACTIONS. AND TO THINK I GAVE HER THOSE ROOMY SLIPPERS!
SHE'S GUILTY I TELL YOU! GUILTY, GUILTY, GUILTY!
IF NOT DOTTY, SOMEONE SHOULD PAY FOR THIS HEINOUS CRIME!
AS LONG AS IT'S NOT ME!
I'D LIKE TO CALL A CHARACTER WITNESS, SOMEONE WHO'LL TELL YOU WHAT REALLY HAPPENED!
THE SMARTEST CREATURE IN ALL OOZE! THE SCARECROW!

DON'T MISS TALES FROM THE CRYPT #9 "WICKEDER"
ON SALE EVERYWHERE!

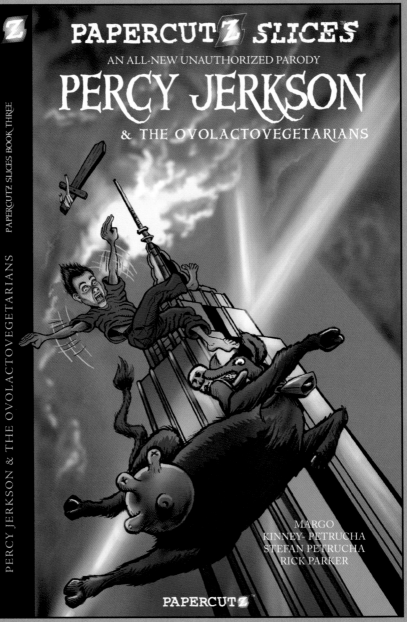